# "ONE"

**Autor: Chesca Luiz Henrique.**

**Contato - E-mail: LuizChesca31@gmail.com**

*Boundless Book Publishers*
*1301 Fannin Street*
*Houston TX 77002*

# TABLE OF CONTENTS


Synopsis: 1

Another Night Of Battle 2

Recruitment Area Of The “Eagle” Base 14

New Formation Of The Recruit Couples 27

Key Explanations For Recruits 35

More Challenges Along The Way 45

Change Of Plans 58

Discussions And Meetings 64

Extra Training 78

The Journey Continues 94

City Of The “Lost” 101

Meeting At The “Swallow” Base 111

Intensive Training 122

Brother Against Brother 134

An Interrupted Training 142

Betrayal Is A Choice And Not Weakness 154

Collective Training 164

Some Tragic Endings Can Have A Happy Start 176

Conversation Update 191

Back To The City Of The “Lost” 203

A Bad Memory 207

The Promise Has To Be Fulfilled 219

An Unwanted Reunion 233

The Reunion .......... 247
Everything In Its Proper Place .......... 257

# SYNOPSIS:

"One" shows the struggle of real couples called "ALLIANCE WARRIORS", where these couples survive in a hostile world to prove that a man's relationship with a woman has a serious and important purpose for human survival and that marriage cannot be described as just any act between a man and a woman, instead, a symbol of commitment, where one has to fight for the other and the two together become one person, one flesh ("one").

This idea of fiction was based on the Holy Bible, Matthew 19:5-6 and Mark 19:7-9.

The history written here is all fiction; but the word of the Lord is true and never dies.

# ANOTHER NIGHT OF BATTLE

It's night and a battle is going on in the desert. On one side, android ninja men and women, they are wearing black ninja clothes and carrying weapons such as swords, axes, spears, bows and arrows.

The ninja attack a group of "ALLIANCE WARRIORS", couples who wear an orange and black uniform with an eagle symbol on the front of the uniform. These couples who are being attacked have their own battle strategy. Husbands have transparent energy shields near their bodies, this protection is done by the marriage alliances of husband and wife, so it allows husbands to fight freely.

Each husband had a combat weapon, either short-range, such as medieval weapons (swords, axes, spears, bows and arrows, among others), or long-range weapons (12-gauge, rifle, shotgun, among others).

As for the wives, they are protected within a transparent energy field and fixed to the ground, this protection was not close to their body, but has the shape of half of a sphere or bubble fixed to the ground.

These wives, through their wedding rings that produced a 3D image and that show combat features, provided assistance to their husbands in combat and every time a wife provided assistance to her husband, whether to reload her weapons, to strengthen or recharge her energetic protection, both wedding rings shone.

Husbands and wives communicated through their wedding rings. William Thompson, a 35-year-old black man, slightly chubby and bald, and his wife, Emma Thompson, a 40-year-old white woman, with a fit body, short black hair, are in this battle.

William, with his medieval spear, fights bravely against the ninjas, he fights using his combat weapon for melee and long-range attacks, throwing his spear at his opponents. Emma accesses the resources of her wedding ring and helps her husband.

"I need to recharge my protection, these android ninjas are not to be underestimated!" said William Thompson, still fighting bravely with his spear. "If they deplete the energy of my protection, that could be the end of me."

"Wait a little longer, honey," advises Emma Thompson analyzing her resource options. "The resource bar for my wedding ring is loading."

The wives continued to study the 3D interface projected by their wedding rings from within their energy fields, so that they can see the combat stats of their mates and the options and resources they have to help them. They can also analyze the status of their enemies.

"Analyzing our opponents, here it shows that many of them are still more than 80% active," warns one of the wives.

"So, we still have a lot of work to do to reduce this capacity of our adversaries," advises one of the husbands.

"That's it, the alliance's energy to use the resources has been charged!" Emma Thompson warns, analyzing her options. "I've recharged your protection field and increased the power of your spear's ranged attack, dear."

"Now leave the rest to me, because I'll make your effort count, honey," says William Thompson, preparing for another fight against the android ninjas.

"I just want you to come back alive."

"But you know how the system works, if anyone has to die in combat, it's the husband, because the opposite of that is his destruction," jokes William Thompson, fighting with a few androids at the same time and defeating them.

"I know how the rules work," says Emma Thompson, clenching her fists. "But everything I can do to keep him alive, I will do. Wives! Total assistance to your husbands!" Emma commands and reanalyzes the options of her resources.

Wives within the energetic protection begin to empower their husbands using the options available in the 3D image. Wedding rings begin to glow, The husbands' energy shields begin to regenerate, and the potency of their weapons begins to increase. Some husbands become more agile, while others become stronger. William Thompson raises his spear and shouts:

"Husbands, fight for your wives or die trying! Let's show these old cans why we are the "ALLIANCE WARRIORS"."

The husbands begin to fight with all their might. William Thompson continues to use his spear for both short and long-range attacks, he also uses a triangular medieval shield to defend himself from the ninja's attacks. When William throws one spear, another is instantly generated by his wedding ring. The struggle continues a little more, the wives continue to help their husbands who fight non-stop. And little by little, the android ninjas begin to be defeated. Then, the remaining ninjas begin to retreat. Emma screams:

"They're retreating!"

William celebrates by raising his spear:

"We managed to win! Point for couples!"

All couples begin to celebrate the victory, wives and husbands deactivate their energetic protections and go to meet and embrace, including Emma Thompson and William Thompson. William Thompson then orders:

"Couples! Let's all go back to the “Eagle” base and celebrate another successful victory."

After William Thompson gives the command, while hugging his wife; All couples start hiking in the desert. Then, they arrive at a city protected by a large wall with security guards made up of couples. In the corners of the walls were statues of eagle couples with their wings outstretched.

The group of couples who have just arrived from the confrontation against the android ninjas meet with other people who live in the “Eagle” base in an illuminated square, the place has a fountain with statues of a pair of eagles in the center, symbolizing unity. The base was identical to medieval castles, but with futuristic technology. On the streets, there were vehicles of the most varied models and years, but all adapted to the desert. The couples celebrate their victory against the android ninjas while eating and drinking. There were also many children who played in the streets and around the fountain. William and Emma are hugging each other, admiring the fountain.

"I don't know what I would do if it weren't for you by my side, especially in these struggles for survival," William Thompson said, smiling and then kissing his wife on the cheek.

"I'm the one who gives thanks every day for the husband I have, even if sometimes I think I don't deserve you," Emma Thompson said, resting her head on her husband's chest.

"Don't say that, my love, you're everything to me. You have always been by my side in my most difficult moments. All relationships have their ups and downs; But it depends on the couple how they will live the happy days and how they will overcome the unhappy days."

"You are right, together we are stronger and we can overcome all the barriers that life puts in our way."

Emma and William hug and when they are about to kiss, they are interrupted by a couple who arrive at the scene. The two wives hug while the two men play wrestling.

"Congratulations, level 15 couple, A rating! You are excellent leaders and "ALLIANCE WARRIORS"," praises her husband who arrived at the scene. "Dodge this punch, Mr. Thompson."

The husband punches William, but William dodges the blow and then retaliates with another punch. William prevents his fist within a few millimeters of hitting his target in the face. William jokes with the man:

"You still need to be faster than that to beat me, my friend."

"I'm going to train more for this, Mr. Thompson," her husband said, punching the air.

After Emma and the other wife finish hugging, the wife comments:

"Emma, I also want my marriage to reach this level and the same rank as your marriage. You and your husband are an example for all of us, as well as the elderly couple too, they are at level 40 and A+ rating. But you both achieved that A rating in record time compared to the level of marriage you're in."

"I say that these achievements were not individual, but with daily struggles as a couple and with a lot of companionship," says Emma Thompson, smiling and looking into her husband's eyes.

"I completely agree with my wife," says William Thompson, looking into his wife's eyes and smiling. "Our achievements counted on the collaboration and participation of both. Always doing for each other."

The couples say goodbye, and when Emma and William return to the kissing scene once again, they are interrupted by other couples and some singles who praise the couple's victory and status.

"I still believe I can be part of the “ALLIANCE WARRIORS” once I find my other half," said a young single man passing by. "You two are amazing.

"I am sure that this time I will find my mate and we will fight together like you, Mr. Thompson and Mrs. Thompson," says a young single woman confidently. "When I look at the “ALLIANCE WARRIORS”, I still see hope in marriage.

William and Emma thank the people and then resume the kissing scene, but; Once again, they are interrupted. William Thompson complains without realizing who has arrived:

"I'm so grateful for the charisma of all of you, but can I spend some time alone with my wife?"

Emma Thompson tries to warn her husband about the people who have just arrived, she nudges him with her elbow and says:

"My love, I think you'd better look back."

But it's no use, because William keeps talking:

"You can leave it to me, love, I talk to these people and they will understand that we need to have our particular moment."

Emma gives her husband a subtle nudge with her foot, trying to warn him again, William screams in pain putting his hand on his foot and asks:

"Why did you do that, love?"

Emma makes a movement with her head pointing at the people who are behind her husband.

"Now I get your message, love," William Thompson says, recomposing his posture when he realizes what's going on. "I saw this scene in a movie. Is it the elderly couple who are after me?"

Emma shakes her head in confirmation and then the two turn in the direction of the elderly couple, Mr. Wilson Richardson and Mrs. Elena Richardson, he is a white-skinned gentleman, 70 years old, thin and with straight white hair, and she is a black-skinned lady, a little chubby, 65 years old and with curly and white hair.

"Mr. Wilson Richardson and Mrs. Elena Richardson, I'm sorry for my lack of education," William Thompson apologizes, bowing his head in respect.

"We are very sorry for this incident," apologizes Emma Thompson, also lowering her head. "This incident had to happen right in the presence of the elderly couple from the “Eagle” base of the “ALLIANCE WARRIORS”," she says in a low voice.

"Don't worry about it, we were both that age one day," jokes Mrs. Elena Richardson, gesturing with one hand. "My husband and I would like to congratulate you both on today's work against the android ninjas."

"As my wife just said, “don't worry about it”. But I need to talk to both of them in the boardroom," Wilson Richardson said, placing one hand on William's shoulder. "I also want to congratulate both of them for today's excellent performance, each victory is very precious for the cause."

"It's an honor to serve the cause," thanks William Thompson and Emma Thompson at the same time.

It is still night and William and Emma are already gathered and talking to the elderly couple, Mr. Wilson Richardson and Mrs. Elena Richardson, in the meeting room. On site, there is a large rectangular table, screens on the walls, and computers on the table. The place also has a medieval appearance, but with futuristic technologies. Mr. Wilson, with his hands folded behind his back, speaks:

"As I was saying, I asked for the presence of you two here, to reinforce the recruitment of new and future couples of tomorrow. I wanted to emphasize that this part of recruitment is very important and we have to be attentive to all the details. Because it is in this initial selection that the new “ALLIANCE WARRIORS” couples will be formed."

Mr. Wilson Richardson turns around the table and approaches the couple William and Emma, puts his hands on their shoulders and continues:

"I also ask you both to help the “ALLIANCE WARRIORS” couples from the “Swallow” base in the process of overcoming. After their base was conquered by the androids, they were a bit disoriented by the situation. Although we have given them all the assistance we can get, including housing here at our base, many are unable to move forward. And despite our efforts to reclaim the “Swallow” base, it is still a very critical situation that we are facing."

Mrs. Elena Richardson walks up to the window, looks out into the street, and says:

"And that's why we need more couples to fight for the cause. And as everyone knows, these new couples need to form on their own; There can be no interference, because when they get married, these couples have started a path where two become “one”, where a woman and a man become one person."

"The most we do is test whether these singles are ready to make this commitment, which is very serious; and not just an adventure as many think," warns Mr. Wilson Richardson, crossing his hands behind his back again. "Young people, adults, couples, people in general; Everyone needs to understand that a relationship bears fruit, and for these fruits to become healthy, it all depends on how they will be cultivated."

"Yes, I understand all that. My husband and I know the importance of this initial process," says Emma Thompson, taking her husband's hand. "This is the phase in which singles begin to get to know each other and do not yet have a bond of commitment. But from this initial process, great couples were formed that can be crucial for our victory."

William Thompson looks at his wife and then speaks:

"And this time, everything happened almost like the other times, We have singles who have already paired up with future partners, but we also have those singles who have enlisted individually in the hope of finding their future suitors in this initial process. The detail is that in the last training of the individual singles, there was that incident that I don't like to remember and some couples broke up because of the failure that gave the system of the “Eagle” base.

"Really, what happened at the last training session for singles who enlisted to meet a suitor, was a tragedy," agrees Ms. Elena Richardson with a sad face.

Mr. Wilson Richardson rests his hands on the table and speaks:

"I also want to point out here at this meeting that the number of enemies is increasing, in addition to the android ninjas on our trail; we also have the android marines who are trying to annihilate any couple that is part of the “ALLIANCE WARRIORS” group."

"I don't understand what drove someone to create these androids, both ninjas and marines, to eliminate couples," says William Thompson, disheartened by the situation. "This is still a big mystery."

"We still don't know the origin of these androids; But what we do know is that androids are manufactured by themselves in their bases. And as planet Earth is no longer the same, the relentless persecution of couples continues," warns Mrs. Elena Richardson.

"The only thing that changes between the two types of androids is that ninjas steal the energy from wedding rings; while the Marines steal the wedding rings of the couples who are members of the “ALLIANCE WARRIORS”. And all of this for some purpose that is still unknown to us, but that needs to be resolved," said Emma Thompson.

"It's like the two types of androids are in some kind of rivalry, a kind of competition to see who achieves their own goal first," Wilson Richardson said with a thoughtful face. "And this is not good for us who fight for the cause."

William Thompson taps one hand with a closed fist, the other hand having an open palm, and speaks:

"But the fact is that the Marines and ninja want to annihilate the human race at any cost. And one of the means they use to benefit from this is through the separation of couples."

Emma Thompson clenches her fists and speaks:

"They hope that the disunity of couples will bring destruction to the relationship. And couples who don't have a daily connection, a constant dialogue, become easy targets for the enemy."

"The truth is that there are many in favor of separation and few who fight for the union of the couple," warns William Thompson in a stronger tone of voice. "And one of the solutions to this problem is for the couple to unite with the few who are in favor of the union and prevent the many who are against the union of the couple from entering their relationship."

"The few humans left on planet Earth do not realize it, but these enemies are trying to annihilate the human species by separating couples, and this has been going on for centuries, or rather, since the existence of the human race," warns Mr. Wilson Richardson.

"It's as if androids already knew from the beginning that a united couple would have the power to face anything, any challenge. But when a couple is separated, they are vulnerable to the world and often follow paths that lead to destruction," said Elena Richardson.

"That is, the enemy uses the force of the couple's union against the couple itself through disunity, They exploit the cracks in the relationship that the couple unknowingly created, that the couple itself created," adds Emma Thompson indignantly. "Then the enemy goes straight to the strong point, making it weak."

"But as long as we have the energy of alliances activated by couples who still believe in the power of union. I still have hope. Even though the existence of these wedding rings is a mystery, it is still our best chance of winning this war. So, everyone be of good cheer, because as long as there are true couples, it is not yet the end," said Mr. Wilson Richardson, showing great confidence.

William and Emma hold their hands tightly and give a thumbs-up sign with their hand, he says:

"And that's what makes me continue to believe in the strength of the couple."

"And regardless of the problems, we will still face it in the traditional way, where a man and a woman fight as one person, as one flesh," said Emma Thompson with great hope.

# RECRUITMENT AREA OF THE "EAGLE" BASE

It's morning and Liam Cooper wakes up scared after hearing a rush outside his room. Liam Cooper is a skinny 18-year-old fair-skinned young man with straight blond hair. He asks:

"What's going on?"

Liam sees his older brother, Noah Cooper, finishing making his bed, already dressed in his orange military uniform with the emblem of an eagle on his chest and a bracelet on his right wrist, Noah Cooper is a young man with white skin, 19 years old, athletic body and straight black hair.

"What's that noise, Noah?" Liam Cooper asks, putting the pillow on his face. "I can't even sleep properly."

"My little brother, Liam Cooper," Noah Cooper jokes, taking the pillow off his brother's face. "I think you've forgotten what day it is."

"My older brother, Noah Cooper, — what kind of day is it to start with all this noise?" Liam Cooper asks in a mocking tone.

"Try to remember, brother," insists Noah Cooper, throwing the pillow that was in his hands to his brother.

Liam quickly gets out of bed when he realizes he is late and yells:

"I'm late for the singles recruitment."

Liam looks out the bedroom window and sees young people over the age of 16 heading in the same direction, some holding hands and others alone.

"I need to hurry up so I don't miss the announcement of couples who haven't formed yet," warns Liam Cooper enthusiastically. "I want to see if I can find the ideal training partner this time."

Noah comments after being surprised by his brother's attitude:

"It's been a long time since I've seen you interested in getting a mate. In fact, the last time we had this conversation about... You know? After the last training incident."

"And how will I forget that day, the day I was betrayed by my training partner? And I want a relationship, but don't expect me to surrender to this relationship like I did last time," Liam Cooper said, starting to change clothes and put on his uniform. "Now I know that there is no such affinity of two people becoming one person. The truth is that in the relationship, it is each person on their own; the couple does not exactly have to live for each other; instead, everyone can do whatever they want individually and still show that they can live together."

Noah Cooper, serious and disapproving of his brother's attitude, asks:

"I don't understand, then, why you want to be recruited? Since this recruitment is for you to find the person who will live by your side for life; but contrary to what you want; Here the couple learns that for a relationship to work, they need to work together, for each other and thus increase the couple's connection and the power of wedding rings."

Liam Cooper finishes putting on his uniform and speaks, softening the situation:

"And like I said, I can prove that one person doesn't have to give themselves to another for a relationship to work. And I know there are other people who think the same as me.

And when I find the right person, a fellow with the same ideals, we will become the best “ALLIANCE WARRIORS”, but without this business of living for each other. After all, I'm not the only one who has been betrayed. And on the other hand, you know that those who stay single cannot have a wedding ring of the “ALLIANCE WARRIORS” and end up staying only with the internal services."

"But that doesn't mean that single people are better or worse than someone who is married; They just choose a solo life. And remembering, that the situation here is about life as a couple, because if a single person fought against these androids without the power of alliances, which is only activated by a couple, that person would die easily."

Liam Cooper, still making light of the situation, says:

"I could also live very well as a member of “Lost”. That is, outside these walls of the base. And so, no android would come after me."

"You know that the 'Lost' are not single or married people, but they are people who live in dishonorable practices with themselves and their partners!" Noah Cooper screams, getting nervous. "They have no commitment to their partners or to themselves. Even androids know that these people are on the path to self-destruction and therefore do not pursue them."

"But I see that they don't have to worry about anything, they just live for the sake of living," insists Liam Cooper, still minimizing the situation. "From my point of view, it seems feasible.

Noah, angry, grabs his brother by the shirt, presses him against the bedroom wall, and shouts:

"They look alive on the outside, but they're already

dead on the inside! They live a life without hope! Do you keep leaving the walls and going to the cities of the “Lost”? A place where dishonor takes over."

Liam pushes his brother very furiously, then adjusts the collar of his uniform and speaks in a stronger tone of voice:

"I just want to remind you — you're only a year older than me! You are neither my father nor my mother! And I'm already eighteen years old."

Noah, calmer, looks at his brother, shakes his head negatively, and with great sadness says:

"Speaking of mom and dad, Liam. You may remember our father and mother who believe in the strength of the couple and who at this moment are out there somewhere fighting androids and thinking about a better future for us and future generations."

"Not everyone has the same vision of the future, brother," Liam said, not caring about the situation. "Not everyone tries to walk on a single road like you, “Mr. Just”. That so-called 'right path' that only people like you believe in."

"Remember, you could end up hurting someone who doesn't deserve it, someone who trusts you. You can get hurt, Liam, on this path you're trying to take."

"Mind your own business, and I'll mind mine, brother. You are not me, and I am not you."

Noah shakes his head, showing that he is dissatisfied with his brother, and asks:

"And how long are you going to play the victim, brother? How long are you going to keep playing the poor guy for others to see? You can dwell on what has happened throughout your life, or you can move on from it and move on. Brother, give yourself a second chance, show yourself that it's not because someone hurt you that you also have to hurt others. You're not like that, a bad person."

Noah leaves the room and leaves his brother talking to himself.

"Don't come and lecture me, the last training was character, if you don't remember, brother?! It took months of coexistence until everything got out of control! I did the impossible for my partner so that in the end I was tossed aside like an old garment," said Liam Cooper, getting annoyed. "And worse, she showed that she would stay with me until the end, but it was enough for a problem to arise and she left me to be with someone else. She only used me as if I were disposable. I don't believe in this business of life as a couple or that one person needs to live for the other! Where is it written that this is standard? Liam closes the bedroom door, sits up on the bed and puts his hands on his face."

Still in the morning, in the recruitment area of the “Eagle” base, single people and couples are gathered in front of a screen behind a stage. All couples and recruits are wearing orange uniforms, some with the symbol of an eagle and others with the symbol of a swallow on the front of the uniform. Among the group of young singles, we have: Anne Smith, a young white woman, 18 years old, thin, with curly, long and red hair; Sophia Johnson, a young black woman, 19 years old, thin, with long curly black hair; Lillian Foster, a 21-year-old young woman, thin, with long, blond and straight hair; and David Miller, a boy, 20 years old, muscular body, red hair, straight and short. They talk in the courtyard of the base, and of the four who are on site, Anne Smith is the only one from the base “Swallow”.

"David Miller, do you promise that when our names come out together as training partners on this big screen, the two of us will only be separated in death?" Anne Smith asks, smiling, looking at David and pointing to the big screen.

"Anne Smith, I promise that the two of us will never be apart again after becoming training partners," says David Miller looking into Anne's eyes.

"David, I can't even think about the possibility of not hanging out with you in this training."

David contradicts Anne, raises his right hand, and speaks very confidently:

"Anne, don't think so, not even in your dreams, because we were both born for each other."

"You're right, if we were born for each other, there's no reason why the two of us can't be together."

Anne and David hug and exchange passionate glances.

"How beautiful to see these two lovebirds together," Sophia Johnson said, hugging each other.

"If I had met David before the 'bachelor with no suitor' training, everything would have been different," Anne Smith said lamentingly. "That way, he and I would have already gone straight to the 'bachelor with suitors' training like you, my good friend, Sophia Johnson."

Lillian Foster puts her hand on her chest and speaks in a joking tone:

"I have to agree with Anne. Because I, Lillian Foster, I also thought I had found my perfect match at the last “singles with no suitor” training. But after the incident, he disappeared, and I never saw him again. He must even be with another partner now. So, I would also like to have found a suitor before the last training, so I don't have to go through what I'm going through."

Lillian has a sad face, and Sophia hugs her and says:

"But this situation didn't just happen to you, Lillian. Many of those who were in this training also lost their companions because of what happened."

"Don't worry, if this is the person who will live by your side for the rest of your life, Lillian. This companion will find you again, whether you want it or not," says David Miller, gesturing with his hands.

"What David said is true. When something must happen, there is nothing that can change it," agrees Lillian Foster, joyful again. "And to tell you the truth, my partner was not the person who gave his best, but he did what was necessary, or at least did a little after the incident happened. I think I liked him, because I believed I could change him."

"We have to be careful, Lillian, there are things that we get signals that shouldn't happen, and we often ignore them," warns Sophia Johnson, putting her hand on Lillian's shoulder. "And relationship is one of those things, because there are many people who enter a relationship without wanting to check the other's past or analyze their attitudes; There are people who only enter the relationship because of physiognomy and status and when these people decide to open their eyes, it is often too late. Lillian, be careful when trying to change someone; that's not always how it works."

"I'll remember that, Sophia," agrees Lillian Foster with an impressed face. "The life of a couple is different from the life of a single person, because in the life of a couple, we have to remember that we have to fight for each other. That now, both have a lifelong commitment, or rather, until death."

Anne is very happy, says jokingly:

"I agree with you, Sophia, and with you, Lillian, too. But in my case and David's, it's already more than confirmed. Isn't that true, David? We don't need to analyze each other's past, because our chemistry has already been confirmed from the beginning."

"And I knew that, Anne, since the last training that we could only communicate by text message and without revealing our name, address, or anything else that described our appearance," David Miller said, putting his hand on Anne's face. "It was a true test of personal character, where each one could see and analyze who their probable future companion is without looking at their appearance."

Anne Smith speaks with conviction:

"We were fully covered with those clothes and helmets... we even looked like professional bikers; only instead of being ready to ride a motorcycle, we were prepared to go to war against androids."

So, Anne Smith has a serious and sad face at the same time.

"What happened, Anne?" Sophia Johnson asks, holding her friend's hand.

"Why were you suddenly so silent and sad?" Lillian Foster asks without understanding the situation.

David Miller speaks by placing one of his arms around Anne's neck:

"You were so happy so far talking about our relationship.

Anne Smith replies in a trembling voice:

"I remembered my parents and the other people who lost everything when our base was attacked by the androids."

"It's not easy to see everything we've built being abandoned or destroyed," said Lillian Foster, also with a sad face.

Anne Smith smiles, clenches her fists, showing confidence, and speaks:

"But as difficult as things were, my parents showed me that the important thing was that one had the other. And when you and I, David, became members of the “ALLIANCE WARRIORS”, we will be able to help in the fight to recover the “Swallow” base with our parents."

"You can count on me for everything, Anne!" Nothing will stop us both," says David Miller confidently.

Sophia speaks proudly of all parents and tries to cheer up her friends:

"And I want to remind you that our parents are also in this fight with the couple of the “Swallow” base to win her back. So, we have to train hard to get strong and make our effort worthwhile."

"That means we're going to have to go into this fight together as well," Noah Cooper said upon arriving at the venue.

Sophia runs and hugs Noah and then asks:

"How are you, my love? Why did it take so long?"

"Let's say my brother and I had another little disagreement," Noah Cooper replies, showing dissatisfaction with what happened to his brother.

"I didn't want to say it, but your brother has become a difficult person to deal with," comments Anne Smith, approaching Noah and Sophia. "He has to get over what happened and move on.

David greets Noah with a handshake, followed by a hug, and then speaks:

"I really have to agree with Anne, there are things that shouldn't happen... Your brother has to understand this and move on with his life. What happened to Liam may have been a warning.

"And I believe he's going to get over it, he just needs time," said Noah Cooper, trying to balance the situation.

"Thank you, brother, for the encouragement, but I don't need anyone's compassion," said Liam Cooper, walking slowly, with a serious face and his hands in his pants pockets. "I've already got my own path mapped out, brother."

"Brother, I don't think we need to get into a discussion here."

"I completely agree with you, brother. I just wanted to say that before I go my way, I want to try once again the path for two, where one person fights for the other. To overcome, as you told me, brother, and with that, totally change my thoughts. You know? I'm going to stop playing the poor guy."

"I can't see your thoughts, brother, but that's the right thing to do," said Noah Cooper suspiciously of Liam. "Because, as I told you, the path you were taking would end up hurting yourself or someone else.

Liam turns his face sideways and grumbles in a low voice:

"And I'm going to go down that path now, to make sure that this isn't the right path for me, and then I'm going to go my true way."

Sophia Johnson, suspicious of Liam, asks: "Is everything okay, Liam? It sounds like you said something."

Liam starts coughing to disguise it and responds by putting his hand in front of his mouth:

"Yes, I'm fine; It's nothing to worry about."

"Liam hasn't been the same since that incident during the last training session," says Lillian Foster with a pitying face. "Poor guy, I'm sorry for him."

"But changing the subject, did the elderly couple arrive?" Liam Cooper asks, putting his hands in his pants pocket again. "Has anyone announced about the new lineup of the couples who broke up in that incident?"

"No, the elderly couple hasn't arrived, and they haven't announced the new lineup yet," replies Anne Smith, holding David's hand. "But I'm already sorry for your future partner, Liam," she says in a serious tone of voice. "The person is looking for a serious commitment, and you're playing this little game of not deciding whether to go one way or the other."

Liam, demonstrating that he is not worried about the situation, says:

"To make sure I don't go down this path of the ALLIANCE WARRIORS, I only need to be paired with you today, Anne. Then I will be sure that my life is to follow a solo path."

Anne makes a horrified face and screams:

"Don't even say that jokingly, Liam!"

Liam Cooper, still making light of the situation, asks:

"Are you talking about me following my life on the path of couples or following my life alone?"

Anne, disbelieving in the question, answers:

"That's not what I meant, I mean about staying with you as a training partner. This is horrible, and I already have my partner for life."

Anne hugs David tightly and continues:

"Only I know everything David did for me during our last training. And I was very lucky to have been able to find him after everything that happened.

David, all proud, speaks:

"I'm the only one who has to thank you for showing up in my life, Anne.

David takes Anne in his arms, spins her around, and then puts her down. Both show that they are very happy.

"We still have to talk about our adventure from that last training," Anne Smith said, smiling and looking David in the eye. "I want to talk about the happy times and the difficult times we live in."

"It will be a pleasure to talk about our adventure, my love," said David Miller looking into Anne's eyes. "And we can start when the new couples are introduced and you and I get back together."

Anne and David embrace again.

"It's been so little time since it all happened, and you already want to remember what happened," comments Liam Cooper incredulously. "And they still keep saying that I'm the one who continues to live in the past."

Anne gets angry with Liam and shouts:

"We're not asking for your opinion on anything, and it's not our fault that your partner did what she did to you! Our case was totally different from yours! So it's worth remembering the moments David and I spent together!"

Liam starts gesturing with his hands for Anne to calm down. He says:

"Calm down, Anne. You don't have to be nervous about small things, and you don't have to offend by talking about people's pasts."

Anne Smith screams again:

"But I get nervous, especially if there's someone interfering with my relationship."

Sophia Johnson points to the stage and warns:

"Attention! The elderly couple arrived."

Everyone stops what they are doing and directs their attention to the elderly couple on stage.

# NEW FORMATION OF THE RECRUIT COUPLES

From the stage, Mr. Wilson Richardson and Ms. Elena Richardson greet people. Mr. Richardson, through the microphone near his mouth, speaks:

"First of all, my beloved wife and I want to thank everyone for your presence. Secondly, I bring sad news to our “Eagle” base. I wanted to say that the number of androids, both ninjas and marines, is increasing, and their attack against our base is at a very high risk level."

Mr. and Mrs. Richardson hold hands on the stage and look at each other for a moment. He continues:

"I still bring sadder news... Our “ALLIANCE WARRIORS” and those from the “Swallow” base are facing difficulties in recovering the “Swallow” base that was taken over by the androids. And couples with the mission of bringing guidance to the “Lost” are having the greatest difficulty of all time. They try to guide the “Lost” as much as possible, showing the importance of a two-way relationship, showing that in a two-person relationship, one has to be committed to the other. But many people don't want a commitment in the relationship anymore. They prefer to have an infidelity relationship, but they forget that this path leads to destruction. And if things continue on this path, the tendency is for future generations to grow up without structure. That is why true couples cannot help but fight for the cause. We need more couples for this fight, because the battle is big and we are few. Now, I move on to my beloved wife to continue."

Mrs. Elena Richardson approaches, stands in front of

her husband, and says:

"I start by complementing what my beloved husband started. We need new couples as soon as possible, but remember that these couples cannot be formed under pressure or involuntarily from both parties; they need to be formed by the free will of both sides, because only then will the power of alliances have an effect. And as much as things are going badly, we need to believe that it is possible to change. Now we are going to announce the couples already formed and the couples who got lost in the last training due to the incident... Of these couples who got lost, some couples managed to recover, others, unfortunately, will start from here."

Mrs. Elena Richardson looks at the screen behind her and, with her ring, projects a 3D image of the formation of old and new couples, she analyzes the image and projects it on the screen. As soon as the screen displays the image, almost everyone is satisfied with the result, with the exception of Anne Smith and David Miller, who can't believe what they are seeing. The screen displays the names, ages, and place of origin of the couples.

Among the couples were:

**Couples:**

**Noah Cooper, 19 years old, training partner “Eagle”, single with suitor” Sophia Johnson, 19 years old, “Eagle” base.**

**David Miller, 20 years old, “Eagle” training partner, single without suitor, Lillian Foster, 21 years old, “Eagle” base.**

The names of Liam Cooper and Anne Smith are at

the bottom of the table.

**Liam Cooper, 18, training partner "Eagle", single without suitor, Anne Smith, 18, base "Swallow".**

Liam Cooper, Anne Smith, Noah Cooper, Sophia Johnson, David Miller, and Lillian Foster are surprised by the result and argue with each other.

"That's impossible! They can't leave pair formation the way it is," said Anne Smith indignantly. "Everyone can see that the pairs formed are not yet the right ones!"

"This system has made a big mistake, we should be together, Anne!" David said angrily, so he looked at his current training partner and spoke more calmly. "No offense, Lillian."

Lillian gestures with a hand, showing that she is not offended, and says:

"There is no need to apologize. I know how you and Anne must be feeling. Especially her."

Lillian looks at her friend who is desperate and then looks at Liam who is only looking at the screen with the result of the couples.

"How can an ignorant computer not see that it has made such a wrong choice," said Anne Smith, still incredulous at the result. "David and I had everything to be together. And look who I'm going to train with now," she looks in Liam's direction with a face of few friends.

Liam doesn't understand why Anne is looking at him. he asks:

"Now, is it my fault? Do you think I wanted to do this training with you? In fact, this situation was not what I expected."

"But you mentioned it a few minutes ago," says Lillian Foster.

Liam approaches Lillian, puts his hand in front of his mouth, and speaks in a low voice:

"If you're not going to help, you don't have to get in the way either. Let's not aggravate the situation further, this was just an irrelevant comment."

Noah starts gesturing with his hands and says:

"Let's all calm down. This phase of the training is just for the new recruits to get to know each other."

Sophia Johnson supports her training partner and says:

"Noah is absolutely right... This phase of training is not intended to bring couples closer together definitively. You heard what Mrs. Elena Richardson said."

"That's true," agrees Lillian Foster, slapping Lian on the back. "You can't form couples without having a connection or under any kind of pressure."

"Sophia and Lillian are right, Anne. We'll find a way to fix that," David Miller said confidently.

Anne hugs David, smiles, and, showing confidence, says:

"You're right, David. Let's find a way to be together."

Then Anne and David hold hands while looking into each other's eyes.

"Love is beautiful," Lillian comments, shaking hands and admiring Anne and David. She waves her hands from side to side.

From the stage, the elderly couple interferes with the discussion of the six young recruits.

"I couldn't help but notice the conflict between you," comments Mr. Wilson Richardson, looking in the direction of Liam, Anne, Noah, Sophia, David, and Lillian. "I want everyone to pay attention. I need to make one more announcement before you get ready for the training. Formed couples who are not compatible do not need to worry, as, as usual, couples will be able to switch pairs if this happens."

"It's true!" Anne Smith celebrates, jumping for joy. "I was so desperate with the result that I forgot this important detail.

"Anne, we just have to run to the teammate exchange area here at the "Eagle" base and exchange the pair of recruits," David Miller advises with great enthusiasm.

Anne clenches her fists, smiles showing that she is very happy, and says: "Then nothing will be able to separate us. She and David look each other in the eye again. David smiles and shakes his head, confirming what Anne said.

Mr. Wilson Richardson draws the attention of the group again:

"I still want to point out that ... In order for this exchange of couples to take place at the stage where you, the recruits, are getting to know each other, the couples need to go to the exchange station. These bracelets that you are wearing are designed to use the same initial skills as wedding rings. Of course, the bracelets do not have the same war power as wedding rings, but they are used to train and gather future couples who are ready to wear the wedding rings and then become one flesh and one person and join the "ALLIANCE WARRIORS"."

Mrs. Elena Richardson helps her husband with the explanation:

"In short, what my husband means is that at the exchange site, you use the bracelets to change partners... However, this can only be done while you are in this phase of training. From the moment they put on the rings, things change."

"The important thing now is that our problem is solved," said Liam Cooper, showing no interest in the explanation. "So, we can already go straight to the place of changing training partners."

"I was going to say that this Liam is an impolite person acting like this," said Anne Smith, seeing Liam heading towards the exchange area. "But incredible as it may seem, this time I agree with him."

Mr. Wilson points his hand in the direction of Anne and Liam and says:

"Just a moment! On that subject, it's the other thing I'm going to comment on, I was just trying to explain the situation."

Mrs. Elena Richardson looks at the recruits and explains:

"What my husband wants to say once again is that this next training was directed to the “Macaw” base."

Mr. Wilson Richardson raises his hand and continues:

"Exactly, all of you will be directed to the “Macaw” base to start the next training, and there you will find the exchange station for couples who are not in tune. Unfortunately, we still have some technical problems in our base."

Liam comments in a low voice:

"I've really noticed that there's nothing working

properly with this training base."

"I can't believe it!" Anne Smith said incredulously and putting her hand on her face. "Only me for something like this to happen."

"Don't worry, Anne," David Miller said, trying to calm Anne down. "We're all going to travel together, and when we get to the other base, we're going straight to the exchange location."

"Friend, don't worry," Lillian Foster said, also trying to console Anne. "Everything will be fine." And I believe that in this exchange, I will find the right person for me to spend the rest of my life."

Anne Smith, Noah Cooper, Sophia Johnson, and David Miller look at Liam Cooper after Lillian has said her last sentence. She starts gesturing with her hands, shaking her head, and tries to explain herself:

"That's not what I meant, you all got it wrong."

"We get it," David Miller said jokingly.

"I meant that I can meet my comrade there at the “Macaw” base," explains Lillian, still disconcerted. "No one deserves someone who doesn't want a serious commitment," she looks at Liam. "No offense, Liam."

"His words didn't hit me," Liam Cooper said, showing no importance to the situation. "So let's all get ready so we can resolve this as soon as possible. And so, everyone will have a happily ever after. Who knows, maybe I'll find someone with the same purpose as mine."

Noah gets up behind his brother and, suspiciously, asks:

"Is that the same purpose you're talking about, brother, to find someone who also wants to give themselves a second chance?"

Liam is all disconcerted by the situation, starts gesturing with his hands, and replies:

"Exactly, that's what I meant. Second chance for everyone.

"Keep going down this path, brother, because that's the right thing to do," Noah Cooper says enthusiastically.

Everyone begins to withdraw from the recruitment area of the "Eagle" base. Noah and Sophia walk hand in hand, Anne and David walk hugging, and Lillian follows alone.

"I'm not going to waste time arguing with my brother," Liam Cooper said quietly as he watched the others leave. "I still need to follow my path, my goal."

# KEY EXPLANATIONS FOR RECRUITS

After the meeting in the recruitment area, couples from the “Eagle” base, “Swallow” base, and the new recruits follow in a fleet of buses. The vehicles are also being escorted by motorcycles with one couple, cars with two couples, and large vans with four couples. Smaller vehicles are positioned in front, behind, and between buses. In the last seats of the last bus, there are: Liam Cooper is sitting by the window with Anne Smith sitting next to the aisle, the two are on the right side of the bus; Noah Cooper is seated on the aisle side with Sophia Johnson sitting on the window side, the two are in the seats behind Liam Cooper and Anne Smith; David Miller is sitting on the aisle side and Lillian Foster sitting by the window, they are on the left side of the bus next to Liam Cooper and Anne Smith. Anne Smith and David Miller hold hands and exchange glances. William Thompson and Emma Thompson are next to the driver and his wife, who also has an exclusive seat of her own.

"Anne, everything will be okay and as it should be," David Miller said comforting Anne. "Soon we will fight side by side as true couples."

"I'm sure of that," Anne Smith believes, smiling at David. "And when everything is in place, we'll both do our best and then join our parents in the fight against androids."

David kisses Anne's hand. Lillian, with the fingers of both hands intertwined, looks at David with Anne, and then looks at Noah with Sophia, and sees the two hugging. She says in a romantic tone:

"How beautiful to see these couples in love."

"What nonsense I have to hear," said Liam Cooper quietly and looking out the window.

Lillian looks at Liam and says:

"Don't be sad, Liam. Our time will come, we just have to believe."

Liam stretches his head, looks at the two couples, returns to his position, and then speaks:

"If I'm going to be like these four, I'd rather not have my turn."

But Liam sees that his brother, Noah, is leaning on his backrest and speaks in a sarcastic tone of voice:

"That's right, Lillian. Our time will come, I can't wait for it.

William walks to the center of the bus aisle and raises his hand, calling for everyone's attention. He says:

"Attention, new recruits and future couples of "ALLIANCE WARRIORS"!"

The new recruits pay attention to William, and he continues:

"My wife and I want to reinforce some issues about couples, bracelets, and rings, as we are moving to the "Macaw" base and I don't want to disrespect or lay recruits in matters about couples and procedures at the base. I want everyone to do well in training."

William looks at the recruits as he walks to the end of the bus, returns to the same place, and continues:

"To begin with, I want to remind you that the hierarchy counts down to the level of the couple, which is marked next to the name on the front of the uniform; that, in short, it is the years of marriage together with the years of combat in the field; The classification of the couple, on the other hand, does not change its hierarchy, since, depending on the couple, the classification is always changing and this is due to their coexistence, it is not every day that we wake up in the same way. But it's worth remembering that combat rating makes all the difference, as I've seen couples in training with low levels defeat couples with high levels because of the rating. As everyone knows, rank helps to charge the skills of wedding alliances faster, helps in attack and defense. In short, it makes a difference in combat. Baby, can you go on?"

Emma Thompson walks up to her husband, smiles at him, and continues with the explanation:

"Continuing with the extrusions, I will talk about the bracelets and future rings for the couples who manage to graduate at the end of these recruit trainings. These rings correspond to engagement rings."

Emma passes her husband in the aisle of the bus, goes to the end of the vehicle, and continues:

"Starting with the bracelets, I want to remind you that your combat level is low, so carry them wisely. Future wives, use the few resources with caution, including the support part for your companions, as resources such as attack, defense, agility, strength, stamina, and other skills are very scarce in terms of how many times they can be used without having to charge the energy again. As for future husbands, their bracelets are very limited in receiving resources, and you can only register one type of weapon at a time. Another detail, as in training and real combat, the couple loses when the wife's or partner's energetic protection is destroyed, remembering that when the wife is about to fall, automatically the husband's ring or the partner's bracelet sends all its energy to the wife's energetic protection as the last act, and so, the husband is exposed, because in these combats, it is the husbands who must sacrifice themselves for their wives; and not the other way around. The only difference between training and actual combat is that in training, you get a second chance; in real combat, not always."

Emma looks at her husband, and he raises his thumb, shaking his head. She continues:

"As I was guiding, after this training, and the couples began to become definitive, you all moved on to part two, which is nothing more than the engagement. At this stage of the relationship, you will wear the engagement rings. These engagement rings have the same status as the wedding ring, but their combat level is medium and their status level is lower. There are some exceptions in which couples end up prolonging this phase. But at this stage of life, rest assured that you will choose well who you want to spend the rest of your life with, because I witnessed many couples give up on marriage in the final stretch to get married. However, those who get married should be aware that it is for life. Therefore, analyze your future suitors well; and I'm not talking about financial or aesthetic analysis, but of character, because this will count for a lot in the future, and at this stage of life, there is no point in going back. After the “Yes”, it is until death do us part."

William Thompson raises his hand and adds:

"Of course, there are exceptions to separating a couple, but they are often very cruel and can bring death. But back to wedding rings, where you become “ALLIANCE WARRIORS”. Their level of combat is high and increases even more with the positive coexistence of the couple, that is, the classification. At this stage, the number of resources, number of weapons, number of skills, number of strategies, and other requirements increase. In the case of weapons, many husbands prefer to evolve a specific weapon and then use others; this helps a lot in combat, once you know your work tool. But back to the subject, it is in this phase, three and final, that you enter a new journey where two become "one", and this phase is for life until death do you part."

Emma walks down the aisle of the bus and explains:

"And I want to remind everyone here that the couples who have graduated already have their proper entry-level jobs at the grassroots; starting with security, where the "ALLIANCE WARRIORS" take turns on the battlefield, at the base's lookout posts and in the armed escort, as do the couples outside with the smaller vehicles. We also have search couples, who have the mission of recruiting off-base couples who want to fight for the cause, but at the moment, we are going through some difficulties, as Mr. Wilson explained before. In the inside work, they can be done by couples or single people. I also wanted to talk about retired couples, but as it is in short supply because of the current needs of the bases, it leaves this matter for another time."

Then Emma gets all excited and smiling, she takes her husband's hand and says:

"And no less important, there is also the prize at the end of the training sessions for the winning beginner couple. The prize has no monetary value, but it is very rewarding for a couple to achieve something in life with someone they love and are by their side for any challenge. We both have our prize to this day. And I conquered with the most important person in my life. My husband."

Emma points to Willian, who shows that he is very proud of his wife. He raises his hands in celebration and says:

"And if today I achieved something and I am the happy man that I am... All this, I conquered because of my wife, whom I love very much. Because she was the one who was in my happy moments, celebrating with me; And it was this warrior woman who helped me get up in my difficult and sad moments."

Emma and William exchange passionate glances, and Lillian gets emotional and comments:

"How beautiful!"

All the recruits on the bus look at William and Emma, the two recompose their postures, and she says:

"Attention!" Let's continue with the extrusions..."

And just as Emma was about to continue the explanation, a red alert appeared inside the buses.

"We are under attack by the android marines!" the driver warns.

When the new recruits look out the window, they see men and women of the Marines, androids in pickup trucks, motorcycles, and cars, all vehicles are modified for combat. The recruits see the vehicles coming in the direction of the bus fleet. The androids' vehicles and their uniforms are khaki in color, they also use long-range weapons attached to the vehicles and revolvers, such as: rifles, bazookas, 12 gauges and other weapons.

"All the wives! All the wives!" - Warns the driver's wife through her wedding ring.

The sound of the driver's wife's voice is broadcast in

all vehicles, she continues:

"Activate the energy protection of wedding rings in vehicles! The more wives activate their protections, the more resistant the protection becomes! Attention! Attention! Activate the energy protection of wedding rings in vehicles! The more wives activate their protections, the more resistant the protection becomes!"

The wives activate the energy protections in the vehicles. The androids' vehicles try to cross the protections by firing their ranged weapons and crashing into their heavier vehicles in the protections. The androids only hit the wards and deal little damage. Android Marines jump out of vehicles and head towards buses.

"Attention!" William Thompson orders through the communicator of his alliance. "The husbands who are not driving the vehicles prepare for combat, while smaller vehicles help the buses. As long as the energetic protection of our wives is active, our enemies will not pass away. But we need to stop them with our physical abilities, along with both short- and long-range attacks from our weapons, before the energy of our wedding rings runs out."

"Wives, attention!" Emma Thompson makes requests through her wedding ring communicator. "Activate physical skills of strength and speed in their husbands. Wives who are helping their husbands behind the wheel, use the guns of the vehicles!"

The couple's wedding rings shine, and the husbands begin to get out of the vehicles and go to meet the androids. A hand-to-hand combat begins. Husbands use the most varied types of weapons, such as spears, axes, swords, 12 gauges, rifles, and others. Husbands also use the skills their wives have equipped them with and can therefore fight toe-to-toe with strength and agility against their opponents. Emma Thompson orders:

"Wives! Increase husbands' physical strength and speed ability! Increase the strength of weapon attacks! Improve your ranged weapon loadout! Increase the durability of close-range weapons!"

"Now that our wives have increased our fighting capacity, let's reduce these old cans to scrap metal!" William Thompson commands, encouraging his group."

William fights more than one android at a time. He uses short-range attacks by hitting his enemies with the spear, uses long-range attacks by throwing his spear and creating another spear in the sequence with his wedding ring. William also uses his medieval triangular shield to defend himself. He defeats his opponents easily with his spear.

"You junkyard!" William Thompson said, removing his spear from the chest of an android. "You're going to need more than that to beat me."

The husbands, with their skills acquired through their wives' wedding rings, begin to beat the androids one by one. Emma from inside the bus and William on the battlefield speak at the same time:

"Couples who fight together win any challenge!"

The couple's smaller vehicles and the androids' vehicles collide, both using long-range weapons and short-range weapons on the sides of the wheels and bodies. The detail is that the attacks of the androids still had to go through the energetic protection of the couples, and this gave a great advantage to the couples. In the case of androids, there was no gender definition. While one android guided the vehicle, the other used the attached weapons to attack his targets. As for the couples' vehicles, the husbands drove the vehicles, and the wives used the weapons attached to the vehicles along with their energy protection.

"The energy protection of wives is very effective, it works in vehicles even when they are in motion," comments one of the motorcyclist husbands while riding a motorcycle with his wife on the pillion.

"This is due to the surface that we have the protection activated, if it is in a fixed place, we cannot move; But another example is about the waves of the sea that we simply let the waters take us away while we have the protection activated," explains the motorcyclist's wife.

"Let's take advantage of this and send these androids for recycling!" said the biker husband, going with his motorcycle towards the androids' motorcycles.

"Count on me until the end! A united couple overcomes any barrier," agrees the wife of the motorcyclist, who prepares to help her husband with the guns attached to the motorcycle.

The motorcyclist husband continues to ride a motorcycle in the direction of the androids' motorcycles, the wife on the back of the motorcycle, hugs her husband and with a controller in her hands uses the weapons that are attached to the front of the motorcycle to attack her enemies, she sees her targets through the camera on the helmet that reproduces the image on the helmet visor. The couple easily defeats their targets with the help of the protection and weapons attached to the motorcycle.

"We did it!" celebrates the biker husband, raising one hand while riding a motorcycle with the other. "Together we are unbeatable for the challenges of the world!"

The couple greets each other with a touch of the hand in the air.

"Only death can separate the two of us!" said the motorcyclist's wife, hugging her husband from behind.

The couples in the other vehicles also start defeating their rivals with their protections and with the weapons attached to the vehicles. Couples show affection by hugging each other after beating opponents. The couples and the new recruits continue to celebrate the victory against the androids, there were pieces of mechanical bodies everywhere.

Then William positions himself near the door of the bus and says:

"Attention, couples and recruits! This was a great victory, but we need to move on, because we are still a long way from our destination."

The couples and recruits position themselves in their seats on the buses and in the smaller vehicles, and everyone continues their journey.

# MORE CHALLENGES ALONG THE WAY

The couples and the new recruits continue their journey through the desert, the fleet of vehicles passes next to a city, abandoned, destroyed, and covered in sand. Everyone observes the buildings buried in the sand, and Emma comments:

"And to think that one day this place was inhabited by a society."

"Now it's just a vestige of what was once someone's home, a parent's job, and many children and young people's school," William Thompson adds with a sad look. "But time does not stop, and we have to keep fighting and surviving for what we believe in until our time comes in this world."

The fleet of vehicles continues the journey, Sophia and Lillian still show a lot of excitement about the couples' victory against the androids.

"Couples with their union managed to beat the androids!" Sophia Johnson said cheerfully.

"The couples are amazing!" Lillian Foster said, sawing her fists and striking the air as she sat next to Liam.

"Noah and I will reach the status of these couples without difficulty, because our connection is so strong," says Sophia Johnson, hugging her workout partner's arm.

Noah Cooper puts on a straight face and disagrees:

"No, Sophia..."

Liam, Anne, David, Lillian, and other recruits present look at Noah with faces of astonishment after he denies Sophia, who also looks at her training buddy.

"How do you say that, Noah?" Lillian Foster asks

incredulously. "His level of status with Sophia in the last training sessions was the best in the base. And the one who was about to reach him was his brother, Liam, but after the incident, the system did not record the score."

"It was good that this happened, because how would the system record this score if deep down my partner already had other intentions?" said Liam Cooper with a sad face. "She already had a suitor."

Lillian is thoughtful and then comments:

"What an irony of fate, Liam. But, once again, you are in a couple training with a person who also already has a future suitor."

"But the case here is different, because he already knows it was a failure of the system," said Anne Smith, gesturing with her hands.

"You don't have to justify yourself, I know perfectly well what's going on," said Liam Cooper still with a sad face. "That's a sign for me to be single," then he smiles discreetly. "But in the status levels, I have to admit, my and my partner's levels together increased resoundingly with each passing workout."

Anne is not satisfied with the conversation and says:

"David and I were also scoring high, but the system didn't register either because of the incident. Isn't that true, honey?"

"I don't remember the final score for sure, but it was certainly high," David Miller replies thoughtfully. "It's just that Noah and Sophia didn't participate in that training, because that training was for singles who didn't have a suitor. But if they had participated, we would certainly be like them."

Lillian comments sadly:

"I wanted to say the same about my teammate in that training, but our status was a catastrophe; I'm glad the system wasn't registered. We only gained a few points in the final stretch when we started to understand each other. And I'm like Liam, I don't know who my partner was in that training after months together. I remember that couples only separated to go to their lodgings, and the next day they met again. Women in one accommodation and men in another."

David and Anne start exchanging glances, and then he realizes that he has lost focus in the conversation and asks:

"I didn't pay attention to what you said about your status with your partner, Lillian."

"I just said it wasn't working out with my training partner," Lillian Foster replies, but when she looks at David and Anne, they're exchanging glances again. "Leave aside what I was going to finish saying."

"Let's go back to the subject before," said Noah Cooper, trying to explain himself. "And I'm sorry to inform everyone, but almost no one could get past Sophia and me, our connection is very strong," he holds his training partner's hand. "And finishing saying what I started, and you all interrupted me." I wasn't denying Sophia's phrase, I would just complement it by saying that we will have a status greater than all the couples present here if she and I continue to fight for each other. That's what I was trying to say."

Sophia is happy, hugs Noah, and he smiles and returns the affection too.

"This couple deserves a commitment score of 1000 points," says Lillian, admiring the scene of the couple in love, Noah and Sophia. "Very cute to see you two with all this connection. As I said before... My turn will still come."

Liam looks out the window and realizes that it is already dark and comments:

"You are all talking, and you didn't realize that it has already darkened."

Noah also looks out the bus window and agrees with his brother:

"You're right, brother. That's not good at all."

"At night, things get even worse," Anne Smith said with a worried face.

"I always felt sorry for the people who stayed outside the bases at night, because many were never seen again," comments David Miller, not liking the situation at all. "And today, we are the ones who are here in the middle of nowhere and at night."

Lillian creates a bit of suspense and says:

"I have heard that beasts that roam at night attack anything that moves and leave no trace."

"So, how did you hear, if all the people the animals found left no trace?" Liam Cooper asks, thoughtful and doubtful.

Lillian again makes a little suspense and replies:

"I just listened, but I didn't ask how people heard."

Liam puts his hand on his face and shakes his head negatively. William and Emma get up from their seats and go to the middle of the aisle of the bus. He orders:

"Attention, recruits! Everyone noticed that it is dark and that attention has to be redoubled. Because of the last battle against the androids, we ended up delaying our journey."

Emma Thompson explains:

"In addition to androids, now, we have to be careful with living beings that have been negatively contaminated. As everyone knows, planet Earth has not been the same for a long time. Living beings have been infected with a type of biological weapon that androids have created to use against us humans. But it ended up getting out of control and turning a part of the living beings into monsters; and these monsters are only active at night because of collateral damage; And thanks to our wedding rings, couples survived the bioweapon effect, while the rest of humanity was not so lucky."

William Thompson raises his hand, calling the recruits' attention to his direction, and speaks:

"I want to remind you, before some uninformed person asks. The “Lost” were a couple of “ALLIANCE WARRIORS” who also survived the androids' bioweapon. But these couples, over time, let their relationships lose strength until they reached the point of living for the world again. And worse than all this, is that they began to reproduce without even worrying about the future of their children or how they should be raised."

"And today, these men and women live without commitment and with dishonor between the couple; they no longer live as a couple should live, i.e., for each other, where two become 'one'," explains Emma Thompson, complementing her husband's subject. "But going back to the current situation, our vehicles don't have power protection turned on, because we have to save energy from our wedding rings, and what we have is for some case of emergency. So, let's hope nothing happens."

"Now that everyone has been warned, stay in your

seats," orders William Thompson, looking into his wife's eyes, and she shows that she is very concerned about the situation.

The vehicles continue their journey through the desert, but it doesn't take long, and once again, the red alert starts ringing. And when everyone looks, they see a monstrous, deformed, and rotting elephant coming towards the fleet of vehicles, Emma orders:

"Attention, wives! Activate energy protection! New threat detected!"

Emma and the other wives activate their wedding rings, and energetic protection begins to form in the vehicles. Emma speaks in a lower tone of voice:

"That was the emergency I was referring to."

"Husbands! Get ready for another confrontation," orders William Thompson through his communicator on the wedding ring. "Use only the energy you need, because we still have a long way to go and we don't know what danger awaits us."

But when the energy protection of the bus that is in front of the bus that William and Emma are on is completed. The monster elephant with its deformed trunk confronts him, causing him to fall on his side, throwing his passengers from one side to the other. But once, William communicates through his marriage alliance with the other husbands:

"All husbands, attention! One group comes with me to attack the beast, and the other group goes to the rescue on the downed bus!"

Emma Thompson communicates with the wives and orders:

"Wives! Use strength skills on husbands that will

help the bus lift it, and the others will use physical skills of speed, stamina, and power boost in combat weapons for husbands who will face the big beast! Always stay connected with your husbands!"

Husbands who are bus drivers brake sharply. The alliances shine, and the two groups of husbands reach their destinations. One group joins to lift the bus, and the other group joins to attack the monster with their long and short range weapons. The smaller vehicles, like motorbikes, cars, and vans, also attack the monster. But the elephant is very resilient and begins to attack with its body, with its trunk throwing some husbands into the air while trampling other husbands.

"I just have to thank my wife who used endurance skills on me," comments one of the husbands who was trampled on, after realizing he was still alive.

"I totally agree with you, my friend," said one of the husbands after being thrown into the air, falling to the ground, and suffering little damage. "If my wife weren't with me in this fight, I don't know what would become of me. Now, let's get back to the fight."

The two husbands pull themselves together and return to the battle against the beast.

"Let's all attack this monster together!" William Thompson orders, raising his spear.

Both the husbands who are in the fight and those who were in the rescue of the bus face the elephant; but the wild beast proves resistant and begins another attack against the husbands; Only this time, his moves were having more effect due to the energy of the wedding rings running out. The monster also attacks the smaller vehicles, causing them to tip over, as the energy protection no longer had the same effect as it was getting weak.

"This is not good at all, the energy of couples' wedding rings is running out faster and faster due to their excessive use," comments Noah Cooper showing that he is very worried.

"We need to do something," said Sophia Johnson, looking out the bus window and seeing the beast attacking all the husbands on the battlefield.

"What can we do?" David Miller asks, showing that he is afraid. "We only have these low-combat level bracelets."

Liam analyzes the situation around him and says in a low voice:

"It's now that I can earn some extra points if I do anything to try to help."

Liam gets up and continues walking down the aisle of the bus. He asks:

"Anne, help me."

"What?" Anne Smith asks without understanding anything at first. "Don't even think I'm going to let you do something stupid," she gets angry at Liam. "You're going to end up getting me in trouble too."

Liam continues walking down the aisle on the bus, and Anne is thoughtful for a few moments and wonders:

"Did I hear what I heard from Liam through our connection? I think I'm going crazy, even with this situation, because that's impossible. And to make matters worse, that stupid, hard-headed Liam is going to do something very foolish."

Liam leaves through the emergency exit of the bus

and goes towards the beast. Noah, through the bus window, sees his brother outside and says:

"I have to do something before my brother ends up dying doing something crazy."

Sophia holds Noah's hand and says:

"If you go, I'll go with you to fight together."

Noah smiles and nods at Sophia, showing that he agrees with her. Noah kisses Sophia's forehead and says:

"And once again, I know I'm following the path of life with the right person. The person I want to have the rest of my life with me."

Noah and Sophia also get off the bus through the window, and Lillian, seeing the situation, says:

"Let's go with them, David. We can't sit here doing nothing while others take their chances."

David complains and nods, showing that he doesn't agree:

"Seriously, this is not going to end well. I'm even seeing the end of it."

"I'll go with you, David," says Anne Smith, encouraging him. "Because together we can overcome anything.

"You're right, Anne," agrees David Miller, plucking up his courage. "Who can stop a couple that together faces any challenge," he sees his fists. "I don't know where I was with my head thinking about negative things when you're here with me."

The two look each other in the eye, and when they are about to kiss, Lillian interrupts them by passing between them. She says:

"Now, enough romance and let's put the plan into

practice. I want to see both of them with that motivation on the battlefield."

Noah, Sophia, David, Anne, and Lillian also get off the bus and follow Liam towards the elephant. The beast is still mercilessly attacking husbands and inferior vehicles. Liam takes the lead by shouting and calling the elephant's attention:

"Here, ugly and brainless animal! Come get me if you can!"

The elephant looks in Liam's direction, makes a sound with his trunk, showing that he is furious, leaves the injured husband on the ground, and starts running towards him.

"And it's not that he's really coming my way," Liam Cooper said, slowly turning back. "I think he didn't like the way I called him."

Then Liam runs away from the beast, and Anne, very nervous, walks towards Liam and the monster elephant. She screams furiously:

"Liam, who do you think you are to go around making these stupid decisions? Do you have no responsibility?"

Liam sees Anne coming towards him, starts screaming and gesticulating with his arms as he runs away from the beast:

"No, Anne! It doesn't come in that direction!"

Liam approaches Anne and pulls her by the arm and the two run away from the beast and go to the edge of an abyss. The elephant begins to approach the two. Anne stumbles and falls into small bushes, knocking Liam into the abyss.

"It wasn't what I planned," shouts Liam Cooper as he falls from the abyss.

Anne looks back and starts screaming in fear when she sees the beast coming towards her:

"Help! Someone help me!"

David starts shouting Lillian's name and runs towards Anne:

"Lillian! Wear the bracelet and activate the endurance skill! That will be enough for me to help my beloved, Anne."

"OK! Leave it to me! - said Lillian Foster, activating her bracelet and forming an energetic protection on her body and David's body.

Emma begins to observe the situation, shakes her head, and demonstrates that she does not believe what she is seeing. She wonders:

"What do these recruited couples think they're doing? I can see it, but I can't believe it."

One of the wives who is on the same bus that Emma sees and deduces, after quickly analyzing the situation:

"I think they want to help, even if that attitude is suicide."

The wives, husbands, and other recruits with features that couldn't believe what they were seeing, see the attitude of the new recruits and see the elephant running towards Anne to attack her. And when the monster elephant approaches to attack Anne; David jumps in front of the animal. David is hit by the beast, he bumps into Anne and throws her into the abyss at the same time as he is thrown away from the place. Lillian runs over to David and helps him up.

"How my body hurts," David complains, walking with difficulty. "I thought that the energetic protection next to my body would be more resistant to the attack of this monster."

"This was the greatest proof of love I've ever seen in my entire life," comments Lillian Foster as she helps her training partner. "I just don't know if Anne will live to thank this attitude like in romance movies."

"Anne has to survive to see how much I love her and that I can do anything for her," said David Miller, still in pain. "I knew the level of the bracelets was low, but I didn't think the levels were that low. We need to go back to help Anne," he continues to complain and walk with difficulty as he leans on Lillian.

Lillian looks back and sees that the monster elephant is coming after David and her.

"One thing at a time, champion," warns Lillian Foster, seeing the elephant getting closer and closer. "First, we will get rid of the beast that is chasing us so that we can survive and then help our friends."

David, still injured, can no longer run and falls to the ground.

"You have to get up!" Lillian Foster said, trying to help him as the beast continued to run towards them. "The monster is coming towards us and is getting closer and closer.

"I can't, I'm too weak," complains David Miller in great pain and increasingly weakened. The attack of this beast was a little stronger than I imagined.

Noah looks at his partner, and she gives a thumbs-up, showing that she is still connected with him.

"Leave it to me, Noah! I understand what I have to

do," says Sophia Johnson, activating her bracelet and activating her and Noah's energy protection. "I'm going to activate the strength skill for you to collide with this monster to knock it into the abyss."

And once again, when the monster would give its final attack, only this time against Lillian and David, he is stopped by Noah. Noah throws himself at the beast, knocking it off the cliff and falling along with the beast. Sophia, with a face of astonishment and sadness, screams when she sees that Noah has fallen into the abyss:

"No! Noah, no!"

Sophia kneels on the floor, puts her hands on her face, and begins to cry.

# CHANGE OF PLANS

After Liam Cooper, Anne Smith, Noah Cooper, and the contaminated elephant fell into the abyss; the group of “ALLIANCE WARRIORS” walks to Lillian Foster, David Miller and Sophia Johnson to help them. William Thompson and Emma Thompson begin by criticizing the new recruits.

"What you all did was crazy and worthy of serious penalties," William Thompson said, gesturing with his hands.

"What you all did was very irresponsible," said Emma Thompson, disbelieving and admitting. "But I also recognize that it was necessary."

William and Emma look each other in the eye and then look at the recruits again and speak at the same time:

"We are very grateful to all of you for what you have done."

One of the husbands approaches and proudly says to the recruits:

"It was a lot of courage for all of you to take this attitude."

One of the wives walks up to the recruits, puts her hand on Lillian's shoulder, and says:

"I just have to thank you for what you all did, because if it wasn't for that attitude, I don't know if I would still be married."

Sophia walks to the edge of the abyss, looks into the abyss, and starts crying. She screams:

"Noah! Noah! I know you're alive, I can feel it. Why don't you respond?"

Emma analyzes the resources of her alliance and explains the situation to William:

"I can't communicate with the bracelets of recruits who have fallen into the abyss. There must be some interference, or I don't even want to think the worst."

"That's not good at all," William Thompson said with a look of concern. "We have to act as quickly as possible."

One of the husbands approaches William Thompson and says:

"Sir, I know these losses are of great importance, but we have to continue and make the efforts of these recruits count."

William sadly nods and confirms:

"You're right, my friend. There is not much to do but collect the bodies."

Then everyone hears Noah Cooper's voice coming from the bottom of the abyss:

"Sophia, I'm fine! And so did my brother and Anne. They're just passing out!"

Sophia wipes the tears from her eyes, all happy, and starts screaming:

"I knew it! We are already going, my love! Don't leave there! Rescue is on the way!"

Sophia looks at the “ALLIANCE WARRIORS” and the recruits and realizes that everyone is watching her.

"What a connection you and Noah have, buddy," Lillian Foster comments, smiling and overjoyed for her friend. "I'm impressed."

"I have to agree with her, because not all couples start with this connection," agrees Emma Thompson with admiration. "The detail is that many times, when a couple reaches a high connection status, they let that status drop little by little or all at once. And for this not to happen, couples have to maintain the connection constantly. And the best way for this to happen is through dialogue and day-to-day actions."

"And I had already thought that they had all left this life for a better one," William Thompson said with a laugh.

Emma, with a serious face, looks at William. He stops laughing and says:

"It was just a joke."

"Noah isn't crazy to die now and leave me a widow so young," Sophia Johnson said, smiling and joking.

"But you're not married to be such a young widow," Lillian Foster said with a thoughtful face.

"But I already consider myself a committed person and more than married," says Sophia Johnson in a more serious tone of voice.

"Now I understand, you don't have to say it twice," Lillian Foster said, gesturing with her hands and showing that she is frightened by Sophia's reaction.

All the couples and recruits in the place look at Sophia. Then, Sophia looks in the direction of the couple and speaks in an authoritative voice:

"And what are we still waiting for?" Let's go to the rescue!

William looks at Sophia in astonishment and orders:

"Couples! You heard the recruit! Let's start moving."

"Yes, sir!" the couples answer at the same time.

William walks up to one of the husbands and orders:

"Take one of the vans, salvage whatever parts you can from the vehicles that were damaged by the monster, and then head to our destination.". As soon as Emma and I rescued the recruits, we caught up with them."

"I understand, sir!" replies the husband.

Emma Thompson walks towards David Miller and some wives.

"Wives, take good care of this wounded recruit," pleads Emma Thompson, taking David's hand. "I saw what you did, recruit. Worthy of a great husband. And that's what couples have to understand. We have to be present in the easy and difficult moments of our teammates."

David smiles and says:

"I understood perfectly about this subject, and I will not forget this very important detail of a relationship."

"Now that everything is decided, we will continue with our new goal and then we will go back to our old goal," says William Thompson, watching the couples work in their roles. "Now it's our turn to act, let's go to the rescue!"

"I'll go along," Sophia Johnson said, raising her hand.

"Recruit, Sophia, you go with the fleet that Emma and I are in charge of the rescue," William Thompson said, trying to calm the recruit's spirits. "Don't worry about your partner, we will take all appropriate measures with them and others."

"It's my future husband who's down there, I'm not going to leave him now," says Sophia Johnson decisively and tapping one foot on the ground. "And I'm just following the guidance I just heard."

"Sophia comes with an agent," Emma Thompson said, placing her hands on the young woman's shoulder. "I would do the same as her if something like this had happened to you, my love."

William smiles and says:

"I could not expect less from a future warrior who

fights for the cause."

David, with great effort, manages to get up and sit down, holds Sophie's arm, and says:

"Tell Anne that I did my best and that I will wait for her at the 'Arara' base to change training partners."

"You can consider your message delivered, my friend," Sophia Johnson said, resting her hand on David's hand.

David smiles, gives a thumbs-up, showing that he trusts Sophia, and then faints.

"Take Recruit David and take good care of him," William Thompson orders four passing husbands. "You two, come with me," he orders, looking at his wife and Sophia. "Activate your flashlights, and we'll use the van to go down with the ropes."

The four husbands remove Davi from the place with a stretcher. Lillian gives Sophia a tight hug and says:

"I will ask for protection for all of you, because those who ask in faith are answered."

"Thank you from the bottom of my heart, my friend," Sophia Johnson said, holding Lillian's hands afterward. "Be careful."

William comments in a low voice to his wife:

"Honey, it looks like we already have the first couple swap coming up."

Emma puts her hand on her face, smiles discreetly, and says to her husband:

"I had already realized this from the beginning of this trip. But it is better to change now, at the stage when they are getting to know each other, than live your whole life with a mistake and not be able to go back. These young people have to understand that a relationship is "until death do us part" and that marriage is not the same as changing clothes. Therefore, get to know your future partner well before making any decisions. Now, we will continue with the rescue mission."

"You said everything you needed to say and a little more, honey," agrees William Thompson, impressed by his wife. "You are absolutely right on this subject. Now, it remains for young people to understand this as well."

The four husbands carry David Miller to one of the buses, where the first aid is administered by the wives begins.

"Let's take care of this young man who risked his life for the "ALLIANCE WARRIORS" and for his future suitor," orders one of the wives who is analyzing David. "This recruit still has a long journey ahead of him. Wives, you must pay attention to your husbands and use the healing skill sparingly."

While women wear their wedding rings with healing capacity on the wounded; William Thompson, Emma Thompson, and Sophia Johnson activate their flashlights through the wedding rings and the bracelet and begin to descend the abyss through the ropes attached to the support at the front of the van.

"Let's go down with caution, because we have a long way to go," advises William Thompson.

As the three descend into the abyss, the fleet of buses and the escort with smaller vehicles begin to travel through the desert again.

# DISCUSSIONS AND MEETINGS

The day dawns, and Noah Cooper wakes up inside a huge fallen tree trunk, he is together with Anne Smith and her brother, Liam Cooper. Liam and Anne are still asleep. Noah talks to himself as he heads for the exit of the large tree trunk:

"That was a good place to hide. I had a bit of work to bring them both to this place, but at least they are alive."

Noah steps out of the tree trunk and sees a giant forest around him. Noah also sees some butterflies and giant bees flying overhead and comments:

"This is amazing! While some living beings have been negatively contaminated with the androids' bioweapon, Other living beings, such as those of the plant kingdom and arthropods, had an effect that favored them, as they increased considerably in size."

Then Liam and Anne slowly climb out of the tree trunk.

"It looks like a truck hit me," complains Liam Cooper, putting his hands behind his back, showing that he is in pain. "My body is all sore."

"I also have my whole body aching," complains Anne Smith, putting her hand on her head. "It was quite a drop."

Anne looks at Liam and changes her face from pain to anger, she walks towards Liam.

"Brother, hold Anne," Liam Cooper insists as he walks away from her. he looks on in astonishment to see that Anne is coming towards him in great anger. "She's coming with a face of few friends," he gestures with his hands, asking for calm. "Brother, I think she wants to kill me, and if you don't do anything, you'll become an only child."

Anne, still with an angry face, continues walking towards Liam, points her finger at him, and says:

"And the blame for all this lies with the 'hero of the moment', who thought he could save the world with his grand plan of an 'irrational animal". I think the chicken has more brains than you, Liam."

"I agree with you, Anne," Noah Cooper said, taking a step in front of Anne and trying to calm her down. "But my brother helped the "ALLIANCE WARRIORS"."

"Did you hear that, Anne?" Liam Cooper asks mockingly and hiding behind his brother. "At least someone here has acknowledged my intention."

"And I could agree with you, Noah, and your brother," Anne Smith said, looking at Liam with a hostile face. "If Liam's true intention was to want to help, but ask your brother, what was the real intention of all this?" She crosses her arms and turns her face, showing that she is very angry. "Liam, you think I didn't hear what you said too quietly inside the bus?" Anne is thoughtful. "Liam, I think you said, like, "This is where I can get some extra points if I do something to try to help". Ask Liam if his true concern was to help or if it was to benefit himself at the expense of others' difficult times."

"I don't know what this crazy Anne is talking about," says Liam Cooper, gesturing with his hands. "It must have been the fall that messed with his neurons."

Anne becomes even more nervous, walks with firmer steps towards Liam, and Noah moves out of his way. Liam starts to move away from Anne even faster, and Anne asks:

"Crazy? Who are you calling crazy?"

Then Anne stops walking, looks thoughtful again, and wonders:

"Now I don't know if I heard you by the sound of your mouth or by our connection. But it couldn't be because of our connection, because we don't have any connection."

Liam signals with his hands, showing his brother, Noah, that Anne is disoriented. Noah shakes his head, showing that he disagrees with Liam and scolds him:

"But once, Liam Cooper was simply Liam Cooper. That person who only thinks about himself. How long do you intend to continue being that person, brother? How long will you carry this pain with you? You have to get over this betrayal and move on. Don't you see that all this is only bad for you? See how you've changed because of it. And it changed to a worse person."

"I'm not going to play your game now, "the lord of reason and one who never makes mistakes," Liam Cooper said, looking around as he walked. "Where should I go to get away from these two?"

"But someone has to tell you the truth, no matter how much it hurts, brother," Noah Cooper said as he went after his brother. "And you have to open your eyes to get out of the situation you're in."

"But who says I want to hear from you?" In fact, I can't stand to hear your voice saying this, saying that, and saying and saying. I want to get out of here now."

"And do you have anything else to say, Anne?"

Liam and Noah, realizing that Anne has not responded, look in their direction. They see Anne talking to herself in a low voice and with her gaze fixed on Liam.

Noah told the truth. Liam wasn't that person before. In fact, he was always cheerful, fun, and with many plans. He always pursued his ideals. What can't a betrayal do to a person? But he can change, and he has to fight for it. Often, our biggest enemy is ourselves, and we can't see it."

Noah snaps his finger in front of Anne's eyes and she startles and stops looking at Liam.

"Are you okay, Anne?" Noah Cooper asks worriedly. "You were talking to yourself and in a low voice."

Liam, not liking the situation, comments:

"And I'm getting more afraid of you, Anne. You had your gaze fixed on me. Now I imagine how much you don't like me."

"Anne, I asked if you have anything else to say?" Noah Cooper asks once again.

"I agree with Liam," replies Anne Smith, still a little disoriented.

Liam and Noah look surprised and ask Anne at the same time:

"Who do you agree with?"

"I didn't want to agree with this airhead, but now is not the time to argue among us, as much as I want to kill him, Liam Cooper."

"You're right, Anne. We have to find a way to get out of here," Noah Cooper agrees, looking around. "Sophia said a rescue was coming, but so far no one has arrived."

"I just know that we need to get to the 'Macaw' base to change training partners so that I can live my true purpose alongside my true love for my entire life," said Anne Smith, smiling and sighing deeply. "David threw himself in front of me to save me, I'm sure he's my companion for life."

"Anne, how did you get here after trying to kill me by throwing me out of that canyon?" Liam Cooper asks mockingly.

"It's just that, although David made every possible effort, David ended up knocking me down because of that uncontrolled beast. And for your information, at that moment I didn't try to kill him, it was an accident. I would have liked to kill him just now, a few minutes ago, if it weren't for his brother's interference."

"But let me get this straight, Anne. Do you want to spend your whole life with someone who threw you out of the abyss?"

"There's no point in trying to talk to you, Liam. You need to seek help to see if someone solves your problem."

Liam begins to imitate Anne:

"“You need to seek help”. You need this, you need that..."

"You're jealous because you don't have anyone, Liam," Anne Smith said, getting nervous again.

"As the saying goes, 'better alone than in bad company,'" sneers Liam Cooper, laughing softly.

"Actually, I don't even know why I'm giving you satisfaction." You're a difficult person to talk to, Liam.

Liam makes light of Anne and then asks:

"Actually, I have another question: how come I'm still alive after falling from that height?"

"Let's say that the androids helped us with their biological weapon. For if it were not for the great leaves of these trees to cushion our fall, I don't think any of the three of us would be here talking or arguing," Noah Cooper replies.

"I think sometimes I prefer not to have the leaves on

the trees just so I don't hear the voice of someone I don't want to name, but who is among us," said Liam Cooper, looking discreetly in Anne's direction.

But Anne notices Liam's movement, gets nervous again, walks towards him, and says:

"Shut up, Liam! Next time, I'll make sure to pluck the leaves off the trees just to watch you fall, Liam Cooper!"

"Like I was saying," Noah Cooper said, standing between Anne and her brother to interfere in the discussion. "When I got here and saw that you two were unconscious, I took you to that tree trunk to spend the night away from the gaze of other contaminated beasts."

"We can't say the elephant monster was as lucky as we were," Liam Cooper said, pointing to the dead elephant, all torn to pieces on the ground next to them. "It's a good thing it's already morning, because living beings that have been negatively contaminated by the biological weapon only come out at night because they are sensitive to daylight directly in the body."

"But there are still other living things that have been positively contaminated with the android bioweapon, because the living things that haven't died and haven't been negatively contaminated, have become stronger and more resilient than before," explains Noah Cooper, looking at the large leaves around. "In fact, many predators are included in this catalog, so we have to be attentive to any movement.

"These living things that are positively contaminated just haven't become deformed and ugly like the negatively contaminated ones," Liam Cooper adds with a worried face. "And they can still walk in daylight to make our situation worse."

"Now, let's talk less and walk more," advises Noah Cooper.

Anne and Liam agree with Noah nodding. And when the three start walking, Sophia, William and Emma arrive at the scene. Noah and Sophia run towards each other and hug each other.

"I was sure you were okay, my love," Sophia Johnson said, smiling and looking into her partner's eyes. "But we had to stop at a cave we found while we were going down, as it was getting too risky to continue down the abyss at night."

"You don't have to explain yourself," Noah Cooper said, smiling, looking into his partner's eyes and stroking her face. "The important thing is that you are here now."

Noah and Sophia hug each other even tightly. William walks over to Liam while Emma walks over to Anne, both to check on the new recruits.

"How are you, Liam?" William Thompson asks, analyzing the recruit.

"I only have a little pain in my body, but nothing that I can't continue our journey with.

"And how are you, Anne?" Emma Thompson asks.

"I'm already much better. Now I just want to meet with David."

"And you two will meet again, we just need to get to the 'Macaw' base."

Sophia walks up to Anne and gives her a hug. Anne returns the hug.

"David asked me to tell you that he did his best and will wait for you at the base of the "Macaw" to make the exchange of companions", Sophia Johnson communicates giving David's message.

Anne clasps her hands together, is moved by what she has heard, and says:

"David was amazing! I know he did his best to protect me."

"I see that everyone is well and ready to move on," William Thompson said, looking at the recruits. "And for the record, all of you will be punished for what happened."

Liam, Anne, Noah, and Sophia look at William with faces of astonishment. Sophia speaks:

"But last night up there, you said..."

William interrupts Sophia, starts laughing, and says:

"You should all have seen the expressions you made. I'm just playing around to relax a bit."

William looks to the side and sees his wife looking at him with a straight face. William changes the tone of his playful voice to a serious tone of voice and speaks:

"I just wanted to say that you are all to be congratulated. This is what we expect from the future members of the “ALLIANCE WARRIORS”."

Emma grumbles, looking at her husband, and then speaks:

"So, now we have to climb this abyss and continue by van until we reach the others or until we reach the “Macaw” base."

"Are you serious?" Liam Cooper asks, looking at the great wall of the abyss. "Are we going to have to do all this?"

"Don't worry, we'll use the ropes that are attached to the van stand to climb up, and the stand is automatic," William Thompson replies, slapping Liam lightly on the back. "And we had to use a lot of rope to get here."

Emma looks at the new recruits and their bracelets

and asks:

"But before we go any further, what do you have in terms of features on your wristbands?"

Liam activates a circular medieval shield on the back of his left arm and a medieval sword in his right hand. He begins to show off with his weapons, defending himself with his shield and slicing through the air with his sword. Liam and Anne's bracelets are glowing.

"I'm an expert in close-range weapons, look at me," says Liam Cooper, still showing off with his shield and sword.

"I have to admit that the kid has talent," confirms William Thompson, admiring Liam's techniques.

"Liam may even be good at what he does, but David is much better than him with close-range weapons," says Anne Smith, showing that she is not convinced by Liam's technique.

"David doesn't even come near my feet with close-range weapons," says Liam Cooper, approaching Anne and looking her in the eye.

"He'd finish you off in a few seconds," Anne Smith contradicts once again and returns Liam's gaze.

And when Anne and Liam continue arguing, they are interrupted by Emma, who says:

"We already understand you both. Let's pick up where we left off."

Liam and Anne turn their backs on each other and cross their arms, showing dissatisfaction with each other. Then Emma looks at Noah and asks:

"And you recruit, what style do you wear in combat?"

Noah, with his left hand, activates a square barrier

from the bottom up fixed to the ground, then activates a medieval crossbow and wields it with both hands, the barrier is made of the same material as the medieval shield and was about six feet tall and wide. Noah and Sophia's bracelet also starts to glow and he states:

"I'm excellent at long-range combat."

Noah runs and hides behind the medieval barrier. Then Noah starts shooting arrows from the top, right side, and left side of the barrier. He moves the barrier with his left hand more than once and without touching it, and then continues shooting arrows. Noah hits the trunk of a tree in the same spot with all the arrow shots.

"I see that we have two excellent warriors in their fields," said Emma Thompson, impressed by Noah and Liam's techniques.

"With Sophia as a training partner and this weaponry; it's all I need to beat my opponents," said Noah Cooper, looking Sophia in the eyes. "And I want to make it very clear that I have reached this stage of skill because my partner has also grown in her combat skill on the field. Together we are “one”."

"And there's no challenge that we both can't overcome if we fight for each other," adds Sophia Johnson, returning Noah's gaze.

Noah and Sophia look at each other with their eyes, showing that they are in love.

"They both remind us of when we were younger, don't they, William, my love?"

"You're absolutely right, honey. The two of us together were and still are unbeatable."

William and Emma exchange passionate glances and

Anne Smith with a trembling gaze, comments:

"I can't wait to be by my future husband's side and look like this, with that passionate look."

"What nonsense I have to hear," Liam Cooper said, making a disgusted face.

"And I can't wait to switch training partners and get rid of you, Liam," Anne Smith said now with a look of contempt.

"That's going to be a favor what you're going to do me!" Liam Cooper screams, starting to tease Anne.

"I say the same!" Anne Smith screams next to Liam's face.

Noah, Sophia, Emma and William watch Liam and Anne argue once again, Sophia comments:

"This will still end in marriage."

Liam and Anne turn their faces in the opposite direction, cross their arms and both react to Sophia's last sentence.

"I'll never want anything to do with that kind of person!" Liam Cooper says angrily.

"I'm the only one who wants nothing to do with you!" Anne Smith said, also annoyed. "Because I already have a better suitor than you and who would die for me."

"And if I were him, I'd do the same thing just so I wouldn't have to put up with you."

"Shut up! Your voice irritates me! Your way of acting irritates me! You annoy me! You keep talking about me, but you can't even get over your own past."

"Now you're talking too much, and I can't accept that."

William comments, putting his hand on his face as a

sign of disapproval:

"These two are like the forehead and nape of the same individual; they never meet."

Emma interferes in Liam and Anne's discussion:

"Enough discussion, let's continue with the report."

Afterwards, she asks Sophia and Anne:

"What do you two have in terms of combat aid features on your bracelets?"

Anne walks away from Liam and replies:

In my resources, I have protection, regeneration abilities, strength, agility, and increased power of combat weapons. These skills are at ten percent in development."

"You can still improve that connection to increase the percentage of these features," advises Emma Thompson.

Anne Smith looks at Liam, grimaces, and explains herself:

"In fact, the two of us are not definitive training partners; we are together only because of the problem in the system of the “Eagle” base."

"And you wouldn't even need to explain that part of the story; everyone noticed that," said Emma Thompson, laughing. "And that's one of the reasons why the rank of both of you has dropped so much. The two of you are not matching, and the classification changes any reaction of the couple."

"And that's the only truth about both of us," agrees Liam Cooper.

Emma approaches Liam, takes his arm, brings him closer to Anne, and explains:

"It may sound strange what I'm going to say, but you're both doing the right thing when it comes to connection, because if the two of you can't understand each other; It's best to stop while you can, because the life of a couple is not the same as the life of a bachelor. I say as many times as necessary. It is best to analyze your future suitors well before making any decisions. There is no point in feeding an illusion, insisting on something that has no future. As difficult as it may be, it is often better to stop the mistake from the beginning than to live with that mistake for a lifetime. And beforehand, there is no point in complaining or blaming someone else for your own choices."

Liam looks at Anne and says:

"And that's why, when we get to the “Macaw” base, we both go straight to the training buddy exchange area."

Anne looks at Liam and agrees:

"This time, I agree with him. And I don't even know how our status went up and down. Our status could not even have moved out of place, as we have no connection."

Emma gives a discreet smile, walks towards Sophia, and asks:

"And how are your bracelet's resource options, recruit?"

"In my resources, I have the same active skills that Anne has; however, my resources are one hundred percent development," replies Sophia Johnson very proud of herself.

"That means your connection and that of your training partner have become very high in a short time, and that means you can move on to the next phase and start with an above-average status. And when you both get married and have your wedding rings, you both will have no problem leveling up," said Emma Thompson, proud of the recruit, and then warned. "But never forget, if you both want to continue with a high connection, you have to nurture the relationship with healthy things and together be greater than any challenge or difference between you."

Sophia and Noah hug and look at each other with looks of love, then William speaks:

"I think we can go back to the van now, we still have a long way to go. The ascent site is right in front."

Liam, Anne, Noah, Sophia, and Emma agree with William, and then they all begin to walk through the woods and towards the wall of the abyss.

# EXTRA TRAINING

Liam Cooper, Anne Smith, Noah Cooper, Sophia Johnson, William Thompson, and Emma Thompson begin to approach the edge of the abyss as they are pulled by the prop in front of the van.

"Today I don't want to know about adventure anymore; we've had enough adventures for the whole year," complains Liam Cooper, showing that he is exhausted. "I'm very tired."

"And to think, some of these adventures could have been avoided if it weren't for a certain person I'm looking at right now," Anne said, fixing her eyes on Liam.

"The way things are going, I'm starting to think that I have to be more careful with my training partner than with the androids and monsters," explains Liam Cooper, trying to avoid Anne's gaze. "Can anyone else here see that Anne has the face of a person who wants to kill someone else?"

"And I can even imagine who the person she wants to kill is," said Noah Cooper jokingly and looking at his brother.

Liam keeps avoiding looking at Anne, who is still looking at him.

"I didn't do anything to get to this situation," said Liam Cooper, playing the victim.

"You never do anything," Anne Smith said, changing her tone of voice. "Are you a totally stable and understanding person?"

"Anne, did you notice how we agreed on something?"

Anne takes a deep breath and speaks more calmly:

"I wasn't asking, but rather being ironic with words. I give up trying to talk to you, Liam."

"This is just a phase that you are both going through," said Sophia Johnson, trying to calm the spirits of the two recruits.

"How I wanted this phase to end," Liam Cooper said, sighing deeply.

Anne Smith, showing hope, says:

"And I am sure that this phase is a lesson for us to learn to value those who really care about us. We just have to overcome the process to the end."

"I can already see in the future you two missing each other," Sophia Johnson said jokingly.

Liam and Anne look at each other and say at the same time:

"It's never going to happen!"

Noah doesn't miss the opportunity and jokingly comments:

"I felt a connection between the two of you."

Liam and Anne look at each other and then turn their faces to the side and sulk. William interrupts the conversation of the recruits and orders:

"Attention! Let's all cheer up, because we are reaching the top of the abyss. To tell you the truth, I would even prefer to go through the forest, because it has more resources."

"But not everything is our way, and our destination is the opposite of the forest on a road with lots of sand, rocks, and a huge sun for company," said Emma Thompson.

Liam's rope starts to move a little faster, and he complains:

"Guys, I think there's something wrong with my rope."

"It took a long time for Liam to start complaining," Anne said, shaking her head negatively. "Don't worry, Liam, your rope won't break."

"I actually think my rope is starting to go up faster than usual."

And as soon as Liam finishes speaking, he is quickly pulled up with the rope.

"What happened?" Noah Cooper asks, becoming disoriented by the situation.

"We'll all find out soon," William Thompson said, looking up and covering his eyes with his hand because of the sunlight.

"That was all that was missing now," complains Anne Smith discouragedly. "If it continues like this, I will never get to David."

Noah, William, and Anne finish speaking their sentences, and the remaining five are pulled with the rope up. When William, Emma, Noah, Sophia, and Anne reach the top, they see a group of “Lost” men and women who wear extravagant clothes showing off sexy parts of their bodies; they are in cars and motorcycles modified to ride in the desert. Some of the “Lost” finish looting the van from the “Eagle” base and flee in one of the modified cars. Two other members of “Lost” have their guns pointed at Liam, who is lying on the ground. Liam has a shotgun and a baseball bat with a wire and nail pointed at his head. The Boss of the group “Lost” walks to the front of his team and speaks in a joking tone:

"Look what we have here, guys. What is it?"

A slightly clumsy man from the group “Lost” drops his hatchet on the ground, but then he quickly picks it up and gets all excited, trying to answer:

"I know! I know what it is! Let me answer, boss! I know the answer."

One of the women in the group “Lost” punches the clumsy man in the head while wielding a 12-gauge gun in her other hand. She says:

"Your hollow head! The boss knows what it is. He is just ironizing the situation."

Clumsy man from the group “Lost” complained of pain and spoke:

"Wow, that punch hurt! You didn't have to hit so hard. What was the boss doing?"

The clumsy man runs his hand over the head where the woman hit.

"You're a really irrational animal," replies the woman from the group “Lost,” getting upset. "The boss was making fun of the situation."

"You don't need to offend either," said the awkward man from the group "Lost", embarrassed by the situation. "At least not in front of everyone."

The leader of the group "Lost" raises his hand, clenches his fist, and speaks:

"Silence! No more side talk! Now, let's get straight to the point."

"And what would be the 'straight to the point'?" William Thompson asks, making light of the situation.

The head of the group “Lost” points his finger at William and Emma's hands and replies:

"We want your wedding rings."

Emma looks at her wedding ring and, showing curiosity, asks:

"And what is your interest in getting the wedding rings? Everyone knows that not just any couple activates the power of wedding rings, but only true couples."

The head of the group "Lost" starts laughing, and his group also starts laughing next, so he goes silent, and so does his group.

"I had no interest in these alliances, until it started to involve monetary values," replies the head of the group "Lost", making a money sign with his hand. "Do you two understand me?"

William and Emma look at each other, and the head of the group, "Lost," continues:

"The things of you, true couples, have more value than the things of the world."

"But only a fool can't see that," says Emma Thompson, crossing her arms. "And at this point, I'm not referring to monetary values.

The leader of the group "Lost" kneels on the ground and begins to explain:

"But, as I was saying, we cannot miss the opportunities that the world offers us. This vehicle of yours, like other vehicles of true couples, is made with a much better material than ours; its weapons are made with a better and differentiated material for proper use with alliances. For us in the world, we can only take what belongs to you, true couples, use what we can, and sell the rest to some collector. And collectors are not few in the world of the "Lost"."

William and Emma look at each other once again, and the head of the group "Lost" stands up, starts laughing, looks in William's direction, and says:

"But an opportunity for the underground market has arrived in the world that is irrefutable."

"And what would that opportunity be?" William Thompson asks, showing interest in the subject. "This may be a clue to many of our doubts."

The clumsy man of the group “Lost” agitated, raised his arm, and replied:

"And do you think my boss is some kind of irrational animal to say anything to you? Life is for the smartest, and he won't say it's the androids..."

And just as the clumsy man from the group “Lost” was about to finish talking, the woman from the group “Lost” punches him in the head again, he drops his close-range weapon again on the ground, and quickly grabs it.

The woman from the group “Lost” brings her mouth close to the clumsy man's ear and then shouts:

"You stupid! You can't interrupt the boss when he's talking! No one is asking you anything!"

The clumsy man in the group “Lost” wipes the ear where the woman screamed, runs his hand over the head where the woman hit, and then complains:

"Now, my head and ear are hurting, you just needed to warn me; you didn't need to hit me."

The leader of the group “Lost” raises his hand once again, clenches his fist, and speaks:

"Silence! Going back to where I was saying. Yes, I'll tell you why I want the rings, since this place will also be the end of the journey for all of you. So there's no reason why I shouldn't tell you what I know."

The head of the group of the “Lost” and his group

start laughing. William looks at his wife, who returns her gaze and then looks at the head of the group of the “Lost” who is still laughing.

"Are you done with the small talk and laughter?" William Thompson asks, still making light of the situation.

The head of the group “Lost” stops laughing and then asks in a more serious tone of voice, pointing his finger at William:

"And do you really want to know before you die?"

"Yes, because I'm very interested to know before you die why you want our wedding rings. For what purpose do you want our wedding rings, and if you know who is responsible for the androids?"

"Then I'll start, and then you'll die in peace. The android Marines are paying a note for the wedding rings of the “ALLIANCE WARRIORS”. I don't know what the purpose is, but there are bad things coming for you, true couples. And for me, what matters is the money they pay me, not their goal. And no one knows the true origin of these androids or who actually controls them. But like I said, if they're paying, I don't want to know who's responsible for them."

Emma raises her right hand and catches the attention of the group “Lost” and their boss:

"I also have a question. What leads you to believe that you can defeat us? If at first we can activate our wedding rings and create our energetic protection to defend ourselves. Not to mention the quality of our combat weapons that you guys don't have."

The head of the group “Lost” looks at his cronies with a straight face, then he starts laughing and says:

"It's just that our number is greater than yours. And I see that here we have about forty individuals from the “Lost” group for every couple, and two of you are still new recruits."

"We're not a couple!" Liam and Anne scream at the same time.

Everyone in the place looks at them with a face of astonishment. Emma puts her hand on her face and makes a negative sign, shaking her head. The head of the group “Lost” points his finger at Anne and Liam and says:

"Now it will be even easier to defeat you six, because the couple that is in crisis in the relationship is the easiest to defeat. In this situation, it is easier to separate and weaken the couple's power, as they already enter a battle at war with themselves."

"I need to do something to get the members of 'Lost' to take the focus off Liam and Anne," Emma Thompson said quietly. "I know what I can do," she raises her hand. "I have a question: how many couples did you defeat?"

The head of the group “Lost” is thoughtful at first and then replies:

"In fact, fighting a couple, my cronies and I never beat any. But we've already taken and sold wedding rings from couples that the ninja androids annihilated, since they're only interested in the energy of the rings."

But then the clumsy man from the ‘Lost’ group raises his hand and blurts out:

"There was also that time when ninja androids wouldn't finish annihilating all couples and just recoiled with the energy of their wedding rings. So we did the dirty work, and then we took and sold the rings to the android Marines.

But in this case, the couples were completely unprotected, but these couples don't seem so unprotected, since the rings and bracelets still have energy."

The clumsy man from the group "Lost" looks at Liam and Anne and, calmer, continues:

"With the exception of the couple who are not getting along, I see that the other two couples will make the fight difficult."

The head of the group "Lost" walks up to the clumsy man and punches him in the head, and yells:

"Shut that damn mouth! We can still win, because we are the majority and we are very well armed!"

The clumsy man from the group "Lost" runs his hand over the spot on his head where his boss hit him and continues muttering in a low voice:

"Everyone keeps beating me just because I tell the truth. How hard is the life of those who are sincere."

"Attention, new recruits! Activate your bracelets and get ready to fight as "one"!" William Thompson orders, raising one of his hands. "This fight we will leave as an extra training for you. Don't forget to use resources wisely, as they are limited. And don't forget to use the medieval shield and medieval barrier, as they are an additional defense for your energy protection near your body."

"Don't forget what these dishonorable people did to other couples; they have to pay for their actions," adds Emma Thompson with a straight face.

Liam, Anne, Noah, and Sophia nod in agreement with William and Emma and activate their bracelets. Liam and Noah activate their energy protection near their bodies, and Anne and Sophia activate their energy protection circular around their bodies and fixed to the ground.

"So, let's get started! I'm going to show that I can win any fight by fighting individually," Liam said, activating his sword and shield, he quickly stands up giving a shield blow and throwing the "Lost" who had their weapons pointed at him on the ground.

"Now it's my turn," Noah said, activating and pointing in the direction of the members of "Lost", his medieval crossbow. "Sophia and I together can overcome any obstacle."

"Eliminate these young apprentices!" shouts the head of the group, "Lost," pointing his finger at Liam and Noah.

The members of the group "Lost", with their guns drawn, begin to run towards Liam and Noah to attack them. Noah starts shooting arrows at his opponents, hitting all of them and knocking them to the ground, while Liam fights bravely with his sword, defeating several enemies in a row. Noah and Liam continue the fight against the group from "Lost".

The head of the group "Lost", furious with the situation that the combat is following, shouts to his henchmen:

"You are useless, attack the energetic protection of future wives! If they fall, future husbands also fall."

While a portion of the "Lost" continue to face Noah and his brother Liam, another part of the members of the group "Lost" runs to the energetic protection of Anne and Sophia; They start shooting with their ranged weapons and attack with their close-range weapons. Sophia and Anne begin to analyze the resource options available in the 3D image. Sophia talks to Noah through the transmitter of his bracelets:

"Noah, I've increased your strength and skill with ranged weapons! So you can shoot more arrows in less time!"

"Positive! Leave it to me now! I'm going to show these "Lost" why they shouldn't mess with my partner and future wife."

Sophia and Noah's bracelet begins to glow. Noah activates his medieval barrier and lifts it in front of him with his left hand, rests the front of the beast on top of the barrier, and starts running towards his companion, he hits his rivals with arrows and with the force of the impact of the medieval barrier. Noah eliminates all his opponents in his area until he reaches Sophia, the two give each other a thumbs up, and then Noah stands with his back to Sophia, protecting her with his barrier and firing arrows at the enemies who were running towards him to attack him.

"Noah, I removed the strength ability and added agility. Now you can shoot arrows even faster," explains Sophia Johnson as she selects her resources.

" Excellent, my love!"

But once Noah and Sophia's bracelet starts to glow, he starts firing quick and accurate arrows, giving his rivals no chance. Noah and Sophia celebrate together.

"We're both a great duo!" Noah Cooper said very happy.

"As long as there is a connection between the two of us, we will never be affected, regardless of the difficulties of our problems," says Sophia Johnson enthusiastically.

Noah and Sophia exchange glances and smiles, and then continue fighting the “Lost”. Liam and Anne were doing well in combat at first, soon the two began to have problems on the battlefield.

"Guys, I think something bad is going on with my energy protection," comments Anne Smith as she watches her energy protection weaken, and some shots from the ranged weapons start to pass through the protection.

Emma and William look in Anne's direction, but do nothing.

"There's something wrong with my combat weapons and me!" Liam Cooper comments, not liking the situation at all. "My weapons have weakened and I'm getting slower and slower. I can feel my energetic protection failing," Liam's medieval sword and shield begin to lose their attack and defense strength, his weapons also begin to come off and return in combat. Liam begins to slowly dodge the attacks and his energetic protection begins to fail.

Emma and William also look in Liam's direction, but do nothing.

Liam continues to dodge his rivals' attacks and then shouts:

"This is not good at all."

Some members of the group “Lost” manage to throw Liam to the ground and then start attacking him with their close-range weapons. Liam screams in pain and communicates with Anne through his bracelet:

"Do something, Anne! If they keep beating me like this, there will be nothing left of me to tell the tale."

"You can't see that I'm in trouble here either. You have to stop looking only at yourself and start looking around you too!" Anne Smith screams when she notices that her energy protection is getting even weaker. She sits on the ground and sees some projectiles from the ranged weapons pass through her protection and go towards her slowly. Anne manages to dodge the shots by moving from side to side within her energy protection. "These weapon shells are slow because the energy shield is reducing their impact, but if it stays like this for too long, I'll become a sieve here. Liam Cooper! Is there a way for you to get up and do something?"

"If I could get up from here, it would be to help the 'Lost'. I would say to the “Lost”: “You can get this crazy woman out of here."

"Do you forget that if something happens to me, you lose too?"

"I think it's worth the risk. Since you can't even do your part of the task, Anne," shouts Liam Cooper, still lying on the floor and being beaten by the members of the group, "Lost".

"Now, is it my fault? But it was you who said you didn't need help. Have you ever stopped to think that if you did your part, I wouldn't have to worry about doing my part? How useless you are!" Anne Smith screams, still dodging the gunfire that has penetrated her protection.

"Sorry, Your Majesty, Anne Smith. I didn't know that you can't solve your problems alone."

"Shut up, Liam Cooper!"

"I will not waste my time and my last moments of life arguing with you!"

"And I say the same thing."

The "Lost" continue to attack Liam and Anne, who do not stop arguing. Liam and Anne yell at each other as the two energetic wards completely crumble, leaving them vulnerable:

"I hate you!"

Anne and Liam realize that their energetic protection is gone, and the two are silent and with faces of astonishment. The leader of the group of the “Lost”, seeing the situation, orders his subordinates:

"Kill these two, now! And don't forget to grab your bracelets. Maybe we'll find some buyer for these objects."

The members of “Lost” prepare to finish off Liam and Anne. They place their finger on the kitten of their ranged weapons, and other individuals prepare to deliver a blow with their short-range weapons. William and Emma look at each other and give a thumbs up; Then your wedding rings shine, your energy protection is activated. Emma selects one of the available resources and, through the 3D image, selects all the members of “Lost”. William activates his spear and throws it into the air. Everyone in the place stops doing what they were going to do and looks at the couple.

"What do you two think you're doing?" asks the head of the group, "Lost," without understanding anything, and looking at William and Emma.

And as soon as the leader of the group “Lost” finishes asking, several spears fall from the sky and stick to the ground next to all the members of “Lost”. Another spear is activated in William's hand. Liam, Anne, Noah, Sophia, and everyone from the group “Lost” who are in the place look in amazement at William and Emma, who maintain a calm and natural posture. The chief of the "Lost" shouts, gesturing with one hand:

"Let's get out of this place!"

The boss of the "Lost" gets into one of the "Lost"

vehicles and makes a threat:

"Next time, we'll kill them all!"

The members of the group “Lost” get into some vehicles and flee the scene, leaving others of their vehicles behind. William walks up to Emma and, with a smile on his face, asks:

"Honey, did you miss the targets on purpose?"

"I decided to act with reason and not with emotion. They are from the group “Lost”, but they are still human."

"You know if this fight had ended with them winning, certainly they would not let us live."

"I know. But we cannot work in the same way as they do. We have to do our best to be different. All of them are on the register of the “ALLIANCE WARRIORS”. Couples have already been called to arrest them, and so the law is made. They responded according to their crimes."

William hugs his wife and says:

"And that's why I'm a happy man and husband. Because “a wise woman builds her house”. And it is not I who speak these words, but he who made the earth and the sea and the sky. Now, let's see what's left of our vehicle."

William walks over to the base van “Eagle”, opens the hood, and begins to analyze the engine.

"I want to talk to both couples," Emma Thompson said, looking at the four recruits.

Liam, Anne, Noah, and Sophia shook their heads in silence, agreeing with Emma.

The engine of the van smokes at William Thompson, and he starts coughing and says:

"Things are bad for us, let's see what we can get out of the vehicles that the 'Lost' left and try to make our van work."

William walks up to a car from the group “Lost”, opens the hood, and starts snooping on it.

"I know you can do this, my love," Emma Thompson shouts proudly and encourages her husband. "You have always been an excellent mechanic at our base."

Emma and William exchange glances and smiles.

# THE JOURNEY CONTINUES

On the road in the desert, the couple of "ALLIANCE WARRIORS" and the four recruits continue to travel in the van of the "Eagle" base. William Thompson drives the vehicle, while Emma Thompson, next to him, analyzes a map with a 3D image. In the back seats, Noah Cooper and Sophia Johnson are hugging and resting next to each other with their eyes closed. And in the back seats, Liam Cooper and Anne Smith sat on opposite sides and looked out the window as if they were totally ignoring each other.

"I've tried to do my best, but with the bad parts of the vehicles that the 'Lost' uses and their adulterated fuel, I don't think we're going to get very far," William Thompson explains, running his hand over his head. "And to help, in addition to the "Lost" looting our vehicle, they also took our food and water."

"Here on the map, it indicates that it has a small 'Swallow' resource and supply base," said Emma Thompson, still analyzing the map in 3D. "It's active for 'ALLIANCE WARRIORS'."

Anne perks up, interrupts Emma, and says:

"I'll love to meet my compatriots again!"

Liam doesn't miss the opportunity to provoke and comment:

"And who knows, maybe we'll leave you with your friends. It can be a good option, and everyone ends the trip happy."

"No one is asking for your opinion, you busybody," Anne Smith shouts furiously and close to Liam's head.

"I want a minute of everyone's attention," William

Thompson said, looking at the two recruits in the van's rearview mirror. "Liam, did you know that if Anne gives up training and you don't find another training partner, you will also be disqualified from training?" The training of recruits is not individual, but in pairs, and thus they form future couples."

"That's what you needed to hear to learn to be quiet," said Anne Smith, still furious with the boy.

"I think I would risk trying to find another partner or giving up on continuing to train," said Liam Cooper with a thoughtful face. "Just so I don't have to keep training with you, Anne," he looks into Anne's eyes.

Anne clenches her fists and threatens to punch Liam, but gives up, crosses her arms with a face of indignation, and says:

"You know how to make a person angry, Liam Cooper. How can you be boring like that?"

"Let's stop the argument," orders William Thompson, he looks at his wife then. "Well, from my wife's tone of voice, I believe we have to improvise on something before we get to the current purpose."

Emma smiles at her husband, holding his hand tightly, and then points her finger at the map:

"As I was saying. There is a city of the “Lost” on the way to our destination. And we could flee the city, but analyzing the situation of our vehicle, I would say that it is better to pass through the city. Because, in addition to our transport being in very bad condition, here on the map it shows that there are many living beings negatively contaminated in the place, and when we get there, it will already be night. What would you rather do, baby?"

"I am with you, no matter what, my love. If you think it's better to go through the city, then that's the city we're going to go through," says William Thompson, taking his hand out from under Emma's hand and placing it over her hand. "And even if the choice doesn't work out, I sign below to say that we came to the same concept together and that we are willing to face the consequences together."

"You know, one thing I always like to say to myself?" Emma Thompson asks, smiling once more and then answering her own question. "You're not perfect, but you're always willing to do the possible and the impossible for me, you're always willing to make it work. I admire that in you, William Thompson."

"What do I admire most of the various qualities you have, my love, is that you are always willing to face everything by my side. Emma Thompson, you are the woman I want by my side for the rest of my life."

"And one of the things that surprises me the most about you, and many wives and husbands don't realize in the relationship, is that you are always attentive to me. Most couples worry about pleasing friends, family, the boss, or even a stranger, but he forgets who is by his side."

"You spoke a great truth, my love. And husbands and wives should be mindful of each other. Because this is a very important part of a couple's relationship. We have to pay attention to behavior, mood swings, and even the way we act. To then enter the dialogue part and see what can be done to resolve the situation."

"As they say: 'It's in the small details that we achieve big results. And I see that I have chosen the right partner to live the rest of my life."

Emma and William kiss briefly, and Liam observes everything discreetly and comments in a low voice:

"So much nonsense in a single day. But my relationship might as well have been like this; But my last companion decided to abandon everything and exchange me for someone else."

Anne does not let the situation go unnoticed and comments in a low voice, but still looks out of the vehicle:

"It's just that you don't know what a life together is, where the two often have to stop following their individual plans to follow a plan for two, where the couple stops dreaming alone and starts dreaming together, where the two work together to achieve their plans. They don't do anything else individually. That's why you think it's absurd, and it must have been why your last partner left you for someone else."

Liam looks at Anne with a disdainful face and says:

"I don't remember asking anything, you busybody."

"But I speak when I want, the mouth is mine," shouts Anne Smith furiously again.

Noah and Sophia wake up just as the argument resumes. Noah still jokes about the situation as Sophia snuggles up to his chest:

"And so the silence that took over this vehicle goes away."

"Couldn't you two stop arguing until we reached our destination?" Sophia Johnson asks, yawning. "I still want to sleep."

"Tell that to the scandalous Anne," Liam Cooper said, looking out the window of the van again.

"You're boring and unbearable, Liam," Anne Smith

said, looking out the other window of the van.

Emma looks in the rearview mirror, closes the map she was analyzing, and says:

"Since everyone is awake and with the power restored. Let's talk a little."

"I still have my whole body aching; I had this fall into the abyss, and then “Lost” gave me a lot of blows because of someone I don't want to name, but that person didn't do anything in the last fight," said Liam Cooper looking at Anne as if he was accusing her.

Anne shows that she is not worried about Liam and turns her face to the side, and comments:

"It was more than deserved what happened to you, Liam. That way, you'll do something useful next time."

Liam and Anne look at each other with the faces of few friends. Emma raises her hand and interrupts Anne and Liam:

"As I was saying, and I hope I won't be interrupted anymore."

Liam and Anne saw their faces on opposite sides of each other again, and Emma continued:

"I think I can talk now." So, I want silence and attention. To begin with, I want to congratulate you, Mr. Noam Cooper, and you, Miss Noam Cooper. Sophia Johnson, the two of you have made a great partnership in the fight against the “Lost”."

Noah and Sophia exchange looks, smiles, and she says:

"All thanks to you, Noah."

Noah hugs Sophia and says:

"I couldn't have done it without you, my love."

"Today should be pampering day, it's not possible for everyone to start with this nonsense of romanticism right now," said Liam Cooper indignantly and grimacing.

"Don't worry, Liam, because today is not just a day of pampering for you, because in your case, today must be the day of envy," jokes Anne Smith, laughing at Liam.

Emma nods negatively and then turns to the recruits and speaks:

"Continuing with what I was saying. Noah Cooper and Sophia Johnson, remember to always be connected in the same way at the beginning of the relationship, because one of the biggest villains of couples is time and disinterest in each other. Don't let your lives fall into sameness; always try to be active and innovative. Now, for you, Mr. Liam Cooper, and for you, Miss Liam Cooper. Anne Smith, you both performed terribly in the fight against the “Lost”. And I, as everyone here has noticed, that the two of you are not having any connection and much less companionship. The two of you are just waiting to get to the exchange point at the “Macaw” base so you never have to see each other again."

Liam and Anne look at each other with the faces of a few friends and say at the same time in a strong tone of voice:

"Exactly!"

Emma makes a disapproving face and then speaks:

"I don't usually ask for what I'm going to ask for, and I even always warn future couples. “Analyze your partners before making any decision, because after the 'Yes', there is no point in regretting”. What I mean is that if the two of you are not getting along, you are making the right decision to break that bond now and before the marriage, so that you don't have surprises after the wedding where you can't go back to the past to change the situation. But what I want from you two, starting today and now, is that the two of you come to an agreement and strive to work together, because if they continue like this, they won't even reach the base of changing training partners. And you can both start by clarifying your doubts through today's combat. So, think about your goals and strive for that goal together."

Liam and Anne look at each other and nod in agreement with Emma, but they still have the characteristics of few friends. Emma continues:

"I know you both understand the fundamentals of teamwork; All that remains is to put it into practice. Or you will both continue to suffer until your fate."

William starts laughing discreetly and continues driving down the road in the sandy desert.

# CITY OF THE "LOST"

It's already night, and the couple William Thompson and Emma Thompson, along with recruits Liam Cooper, Anne Smith, Noah Cooper, and Sophia Johnson, continue their journey through the desert in the van of the "Eagle" base.

"There's something weird going on," Emma said, scanning the map with the 3D image.

"What's wrong, honey?"

"William, my dear, at this distance, we should already be seeing the light of the city of the 'Lost'. I'm not bragging, but I don't usually make mistakes when I analyze these maps."

"And I don't doubt you, my dear, because you've already taken our battalion out of many life-and-death situations, guiding us like a compass."

"Everything in this life has its first time," Liam Cooper said mockingly.

"Now, I know what you're going through, Anne," Emma Thompson said, looking at Liam in the rearview mirror. "And Liam, I didn't say I never made a mistake. I said that I don't usually make mistakes when I'm analyzing a map. There is a difference between one thing and another.

"I say Liam is hard to deal with, but you all think I'm exaggerating," Anne Smith complains, grimacing at Liam. "Not only does Liam not help at all, but he also hinders everything else."

Liam looks out the window and says:

"I will say nothing more from this moment on. You will no longer hear my voice."

Anne, Noah, Sophia, William, and Emma begin to celebrate in front of Liam after what he said.

Noah looks at Liam and says jokingly:

"Brother, now I believe that all is not lost. As they say, “Hope is the last thing that dies."

"That's something, Liam," Sophia Johnson said mockingly. "From the moment you made that decision on your own, you've already done a lot for the whole team."

"What Sophia means is that this attitude of yours, Liam. It's one less thing for the team to worry about," Anne Smith said mockingly and close to Liam's face.

"Get away from me, Anne," Liam Cooper insists, pushing Anne's face away from him. "Since you're all funny, you should work in a circus. But I'll say something for you all to know..."

And just as Liam is about to continue with his speech, William brakes the van sharply and stops close to the wall made of tree trunks in the city of the “Lost”. Everyone inside the van screams, and then the occupants of the van pull themselves together.

"You bought your driver's license," Liam Cooper complains with a scared face. "If it continues like this, it will end up killing everyone here."

"I actually got my driver's license while I was still training to become one of the 'ALLIANCE WARRIORS, '" replies William Thompson.

"We were saved from yet another Liam Cooper speech by William Thompson, who made a risky maneuver to save everyone from this conversation," Anne Smith said jokingly.

"Anne, the conversation hasn't reached you yet. You

can be quiet," said Liam Cooper, raising his hand in front of Anne's mouth, who would try to say something. "I'm not done yet. And I wasn't asking a question, but a critique of where you got your license to drive, Mr. Thompson."

"Now I understand, you should have been more specific, Liam," William Thompson said, downplaying the conversation with Liam.

Liam was about to start talking, but was interrupted by his brother Noah:

"Liam, brother, remember your promise."

"Liam, for everyone's sake, please keep the promise you just made," implores Sophia Johnson, covering her ears with her hand. "I can't stand to hear you complaining anymore."

Liam sulks and asks:

"Am I the only one who's wrong here? But is no one wrong?"

William, Emma, Anne, Noah, and Sophia respond at the same time:

"Yes!"

Liam sulks and is silent, looking out the window of the van.

"Attention! Something is not right in this town," orders Emma Thompson suspiciously. "The city of the 'Lost' is usually very busy at night.

"We're going to drive through the city and follow our destination," said William Thompson, who drives and follows the wall made of tree trunks. "It's not wise to stay in a lawless place for too long," he enters through the city's main gate and drives down the main street.

"Very strange that this place is deserted like this,

because here in the report I took of the place, it shows that this place is being inhabited," said Emma Thompson, looking out the window of the van and seeing the empty city.

Liam points his finger out of the van and catches the attention of everyone in the vehicle:

"Look outside!" There's something strange out there.

"Are you going to start over, Liam?" Anne Smith asks, putting her hand on her face as a sign of disapproval of Liam's attitude.

"Now is not the time to complain, brother," Noah Cooper said in a more serious tone of voice. "We are in enemy territory.

"Liam, listen to your brother this time," said Sophia Johnson, seeing the city without people.

"But I'm serious," Liam Cooper shouts, raising his voice. "Just stop criticizing me and look outside," he says, a little calmer.

William looks in the direction Liam is showing and says:

"This time, Liam is right. Look outside!"

William maneuvers the car, turns on the van's high light, and everyone sees the bodies of android ninjas, android marines, and people from the "Lost" group torn apart and strewn across the city's streets and sidewalks.

"Who or what did it?" Emma Thompson asks, not believing what she is seeing.

"What or who did it I don't know; but it not only attacked the "Lost", but also eliminated the ninjas and marines," said Sophia Johnson, showing concern about the situation.

"That means the thing or things that did it are very

strong," comments Noah Cooper, still looking at the torn bodies.

"Let's take a closer look and move on," William Thompson said, shutting down the van.

"I don't know if it's a good idea to get out of the van," said Liam Cooper, looking from inside the vehicle at the torn bodies apart and becoming uncomfortable with the situation. "And I'm not in a position to fight, so I won't be able to help at all if something goes wrong."

And before Liam even finishes speaking, everyone opens the doors and gets out of the van. Liam nods and comments to himself:

"I don't think any of you should ignore what I just said at this point."

Anne outside the van, looks at Liam and asks in a mocking tone:

"And who said your opinion is relevant, Liam? You're just embarrassing yourself."

Liam looks around once again and with a worried face, says:

"Anne, don't play with anything serious. Then something terrible happens, they will say that I am the one who keeps talking a lot. I don't think it's a good idea to stay here in the city where the banquet is served. And I assure you that this banquet that is already served, is not for us, of that I am sure."

Anne next to the van and near the door where Liam is, observes the place and speaks:

"Even on these occasions you complain, Liam. How can you be like that?"

Liam opens the door of the vehicle and without

leaving the seat, looks around and then looks at Anne and says:

"As far as I know, we're not a very big number, we don't have a lot of energy in the rings or the bracelets. And not to mention that the thing or things that did it, did it to the androids as well. Imagine what he wouldn't do to us too. I just think that first, we should seek help."

Anne looks around once again and seeing the bodies scattered on the streets and sidewalks of the city, says:

"I hate to have to agree with you, Liam. But this time, I'm forced to admit it. We are not in a position to fight anyone. If only David was here with me."

Liam puts his hand on his face disapproving and says:

"I don't believe David would make all the difference you're mentioning."

"But I know what David would do for me," said Anne Smith, showing that she is in love. "Only he and I know the difficulties we went through in the last training sessions."

Liam shakes his head in disbelief at what he is hearing from Anne and warns:

"Be careful, Anne. Those who live a lot of fiction end up not living the true reality."

"You're jealous because I have someone to fight for and someone to fight for me," says Anne Smith, changing her tone of voice from passionate to angry.

As Liam and Anne start another argument, William and Emma walk to the next block of Main Street, where they see more bodies of ninjas, Marines, and people from the "Lost" group torn apart.

"Everything indicates that it was some kind of

predator that did this atrocity," William Thompson deduces, analyzing one of the bodies. "I know that these living beings affected by the biological weapon of the androids are very aggressive, but not to the point of invading a city."

"Something happened to these living things to make them reach this level of ferocity," Emma Thompson said, seeing chain marks on the ground, she shows her husband. "Look at that. Let's follow this trail of currents and see where it takes us."

The two begin to follow the trail that leads them to a large cage that is open in the main square of the city. William and Emma begin to analyze the place.

"But what is that?" William Thompson asks, impressed by the structure.

"Look at those claw marks. Apparently, someone captured a supposed negatively contaminated living being," replies Emma Thompson by analyzing claw marks on the cage and deducing. "The beast must have escaped, and this atrocity that we are witnessing happened."

William puts his hand on his chin and says:

"Now we need to find out why someone is going to capture negatively contaminated living beings."

Then, Sophia and Noah, who are on the other block of Main Street, start gesturing with their arms to get the attention of the others.

"Run here!" shouts Sophia Johnson.

"There's something you need to see!" Noah Cooper screams.

William and Emma arrive at the scene and see the bodies of a couple of the “ALLIANCE WARRIORS” from the “Swallow” base at the site. There were bodies of couples scattered everywhere. William and Emma are outraged by what they are seeing.

"But what the hell happened here?" Emma Thompson asks, outraged by what she is seeing.

"Everything indicates that couples have gathered here to face whatever it is, but they couldn't win," deduces William Thompson, incredulous at what he is witnessing. "Before heading to our destination at the “Swallow” base. We will have to find out what is happening in this place.

"I don't know what drove someone to bring a monster into this town, but I think I already know where we can find answers," said Emma Thompson, clenching her fists and looking at the couples in orange uniforms and with swallow symbols on their chests.

Liam and Anne, still afraid of the place they are in, continue to observe everything around, she next to the vehicle and he from inside the vehicle.

"Anne, because I don't think they should be making that much noise here."

"Even though it's very difficult, I need to agree with you once again, Liam."

"I imagine how it must be."

Then, Emma, William, Noah, Sophia, Liam, and Anne hear a roar near where they are.

"It's time for us to go," warns Emma Thompson.

"I don't think it would be a good time to fight anybody at this point," William Thompson said, concerned about the situation. "Unless it was very necessary."

"But we will find those responsible for this atrocity," says Emma Thompson with a face of few friends. "That I am sure of."

William, Emma, Noah and Sophia rush to the van. Everyone quickly gets into the van when they hear the roar again and even closer. Anne jumps on Liam's lap at the same time as he pulls her inside. Liam closes the door quickly. William starts the vehicle and leaves the city as soon as possible. Everyone looks in amazement at Anne, who is on Liam's lap.

"It was all so fast that I didn't even see that I pulled her into the car," Liam said, trying to explain himself.

"I heard the roar and saw you running, I didn't know what to do," Anne Smith said, trying to explain herself. "So I jumped in the car as fast as I could."

Emma, Noah, Sophia, and William continue to look at the two still with faces of astonishment. William looks in the vehicle's rearview mirror and drives at the same time. Liam and Anne quickly break up when they realize they were still together, the two try to explain themselves once again.

"As Liam said, it was all so fast," said Anne Smith trying to explain herself once again. "That's not what you're thinking," she gestures with her hands.

"I agree with Anne," Liam said, not knowing what to do. "When it comes to adrenaline and everyone having to run away, we end up doing things without thinking."

Sophia and Noah look suspiciously at each other with the situation, and Sophia, surprised, asks:

"Are you two agreeing with each other?"

"This is what I'm seeing, but my eyes don't want to believe it." Noah Cooper jokingly asks.

"I just want to get to my purpose; and I believe Liam did too," said Anne Smith, taking a deep breath. "Right,

Liam?" She asks looking down.

Liam looks at Anne with a fixed gaze. Anne waits for Liam to respond. And once again, everyone inside the van looks at the two of them. Anne nudges Liam with her hand, and he acts, not knowing what to say:

"Yes, that's right. Anne is right, or not. I don't know what to answer at this point, that's the truth."

"I think it's best for all of us to focus on the situation at the moment," Emma Thompson said, interrupting. "And the situation doesn't seem friendly at all."

"We'll see what we find out when we get to the 'Swallow' base," William Thompson said as he drove the van.

The couple and the four recruits follow in the van through the desert.

# MEETING AT THE “SWALLOW” BASE

It's still night, and Liam Cooper, Anne Smith, Noah Cooper, Sophia Johnson, William Thompson, and Emma Thompson, with the van from the “Eagle” base, are on their way to the “Swallow” base. They can already see the base lights a little far away.

"We're already arriving, look at our current destination ahead," says Emma Thompson.

"It looks like we can now regain our strength and try to better understand what's going on in this area," William Thompson said.

The six arrive at the main gate of the “Swallow” base. In the corners of the base walls were statues of couples of swallows with their wings spread. On the large walls of the base, there were also couples, where husbands wielded rifles and laser-sighted bows and arrows, while wives analyzed the situation through 3D images. All the husbands had their guns pointed at the van at the “Eagle” base. Emma realizes that she has red spots on her body, on the bodies of others and screams:

"William, stop the vehicle! We are in their sights."

William hears his wife slam on the brakes, and the van even skids to the side, raising a lot of dust. The six inside the vehicle are motionless and with their hands up. William is just moving his lips, he advises:

"Nobody makes sudden movements, let's wait for the reconnaissance team of the “Swallow” base to do the inspection."

The elderly couple, Nicholas Henderson and Jennifer

Henderson, from the “ALLIANCE WARRIORS” of the “Swallow” base, climbs the wall and stands next to the base guards, he is a 60-year-old black man, thin body, short white hair; She, a 65-year-old white lady, chubby body, long white hair.

Mr. Nicholas points his rifle with laser sights at the van. At the end of his rifle was an adapted bayonet. Ms. Jennifer wears her wedding ring and analyzes the van and its passengers through the information gathered by her husband's telescopic sight that was transmitted to the 3D image. The image shows all the occupants of the van and their technical sheets. Then, Jennifer orders:

"Let them in! They are “ALLIANCE WARRIORS” from the “Eagle” base and are together with one of ours."

Mr. Nicholas puts his rifle into rest mode and shouts with joy:

"They are allies! Give them the signal to come in! Open the main gate! I want all of them in my living room and very well served."

A couple standing at the main gate starts flashing a light, and then the gate starts opening.

"They've done our analysis and we can move on," said Emma Thompson, more relieved. "These reconnaissance analyses are important, as the androids have already tried to invade bases infiltrated in vehicles of the 'ALLIANCE WARRIORS'."

"You have to be very careful when it's wartime," William Thompson adds, turning on the van. "Let's go ahead," he heads to the main entrance of the “Swallow” base.

As soon as the vehicle passes through the gate, it begins to close. William, his wife, and the four recruits are greeted with great joy by the people of the place, even before they get out of the vehicle.

In a corridor of the "Swallow" base, Liam Cooper, Anne Smith, Noah Cooper, Sophia Johnson, William Thompson, and Emma Thompson are guided by a couple of "ALLIANCE WARRIORS" to the door that gives access to the meeting room. As soon as everyone reaches the door, some guards open it so that only the six guests can get through. They are greeted with great joy by the elderly couple, Nicholas Henderson and Jennifer Henderson. There was a table with lots of drinks and food on site.

"My friends, Mr. William Thompson and Mrs. Emma Thompson, welcome along with your people," Nicolas Henderson said, giving William a hug, taking Emma's hand, and greeting her. "My house is your home.

"It is a pleasure to see my old combat comrades, Mr. Nicholas Henderson and Mrs. Jennifer Henderson," William Thompson said, taking Jennifer's hand and greeting her. "How long has it been since I saw them?"

"What a joy to have you here," Jennifer Henderson said, hugging Emma and then rubbing the faces of the four recruits fondly. "You don't know how happy I am to receive friends of the same cause in my humble residence. I'm sure it was a tiring trip for all of you."

Emma walks behind the four recruits and then speaks:

"Yes, it was a battle for us to get here, and we still have a long way to go. But I am very grateful that we all made it this far alive. And yet, having this wonderful reception. Sometimes, what is missing in our lives is to thank more, much more; and complain less, much less."

"I know what it's like, my friend," agrees Jennifer Henderson, looking dejected. "Sometimes we want to see the future, But we don't even look at where we are stepping in the present."

Then Jennifer looks and walks towards Anne, who does the same, the two hug each other with tears in their eyes, and Jennifer comments:

"How are you, my dear, Anne? In my point of view, you are much bigger than the last time I saw you."

"I'm much better now that we've arrived here. I'm still in the training process. I can't wait to join the "ALLIANCE WARRIORS" to help fight for the cause, including to help my parents regain the main base "Swallow"."

Jennifer looks in the direction of the other recruits, analyzing them, and then comments:

"And seeing the couples here, do I believe this should be your future husband?"

Jennifer points to Liam.

Liam, Anne, Noah, Sophia, William, and Emma look at each other, and just as Emma was about to speak, Anne takes control of the situation, looks at Liam, and replies:

"Liam and I will stay together until we make the switch at the "Swallow" base." There was a small unforeseen event in the last few days that ended up as things are. But it's nothing that can't be solved, Ms. Jennifer Henderson.

"I understand when a couple still in formation already realizes that they have no future and seeks the best for both. And this is very important. In the phase of knowing who you want to live with your whole life, you still have the option of separating; because this option of separation for those who know the importance of a marriage; This can only be done before marriage. After the wedding is another story."

"And we are already well aware of this, as our leader, Mrs. Emma Thompson, reminds us all the time about the importance of marriage," Sophia Johnson said, making a heart sign with her hands to Emma.

"And I'm grateful to have Mr. William Thompson and Mrs. Emma Thompson as our instructors, because there is often a lack of instructors who bring quality knowledge to young people," adds Noah Cooper, giving a thumbs-up to William.

William and Emma look at each other, return the gestures to the two recruits and give a discreet smile.

"And we're both very happy to see that our efforts are paying off," William Thompson said proudly. "I'm happy to see this kind of result.

"It's very gratifying to see what we're fighting for, reaching out to the next generation of young people," said Emma Thompson, emotional and wiping tears from her eyes. "It is very gratifying to see that what was done at the beginning still lives."

Nicholas Henderson walks up to Anne, puts his hands on her shoulder and says:

"Talking about the main base; it's not just you, my young lady, but my wife and I also need to join the other “ALLIANCE WARRIORS” from the “Swallow” base and those from the “Eagle” base, who are also in the fight with us in search of victory. But now, we are at war here as well, and this small “Swallow” base is a strong strategy for our allies who come to replenish their forces. And that's why we can't lose that base."

"But, after all, what is happening in this area?" William Thompson asks, trying to understand the situation. "We saw bodies scattered around the city of the 'Lost', including bodies of couples of the 'ALLIANCE WARRIORS'."

"Before we get into this conversation, you all eat first and shower, while we pack up your uniforms and then gather here to talk," Nicholas Henderson said, placing his hand on William's shoulder. "We are living in difficult times."

"And I also want more details about what happened to Anne and Liam, I want to understand why they both want to change training partners so badly," Jennifer Henderson said, putting her hands on the shoulders of the two recruits.

Anne and Liam look at each other, and Anne says:

"It's not a very happy story, but I believe it will have a happy ending."

Liam looks at the floor with a sad face as everyone walks towards the table to eat.

"This feast seems to be very tasty," Noah Cooper deduces, looking at a table full of food. "Come on, Liam! If you stay in this place, you will not eat."

Liam, to his brother, smiles, runs towards the table, and says:

"You won't start eating without me!"

After a while, Liam, Anne, Noah, Sophia, William, Emma, Nicholas, and Jennifer are already gathered in the meeting room again. Liam, Anne, Noah, Sophia, William, and Emma have their uniforms cleaned, and the table with the banquet is already empty. They're all sitting around the table as a couple.

"I hope everyone is satisfied with the banquet that has

been served," said Nicholas Henderson, gesturing with his hands.

"I can't complain about anything; everything was very good," said Liam Cooper, running his hand over his belly. "Now it's just a matter of getting a very cozy place to sleep."

Anne looks at Liam indignantly and says:

"It wasn't a direct question for you, Liam. And no one is asking you where you want to sleep."

"I'm just being polite, Anne."

"It was already taking a long time for the two of them to start arguing," Noah Cooper said jokingly.

"And I thought Liam and Anne were getting along," says Sophia Johnson, laughing. "Only I think about such a thing."

"There's no talking to Liam, he doesn't change the way he acts," Anne Smith said, taunting her training partner. "He likes to attract attention."

"The two can postpone this discussion for another time, because we now have very important issues to deal with," William Thompson said, intervening in the discussion. "And this is not a request, but an order."

"And we can get straight to the point about what's going on in this area, because I've already talked to Anne about the reason for the exchange that Liam and she will have to make, and I've already warned my husband about the situation," adds Jennifer Henderson.

"Yes, my wife has already told me about the unforeseen event that happened at the "Eagle" base. Our new recruits have also left for the "Macaw" base, because their training base is more complete than the one we have here," said Nicholas Henderson, holding his wife's hand.

"Almost all of the recruited couples have left, with the exception of one couple, who are having a little bit of difficulty with training, but we'll leave that conversation for another time," adds Jennifer Henderson.

Nicholas looks at Anne and Liam, puts his hand on his chin, gets a little thoughtful, and his wife asks:

"Any problem, honey?"

"No, but I wanted to leave something on record between us. Because when I looked at you two in the beginning, I thought you were a great couple and that you had a lot of future together."

Anne and Liam look at each other and then turn their faces to opposite sides.

"Appearances can be deceiving, Mr. Henderson," said Anne Smith, showing her discomfort with the conversation. "And I already have my suitor, and I don't intend to give up on him, especially because of the number of things he and I went through together in the last training," she crosses her arms. "I know he would die for me, because he showed it so many times. We were both made for each other."

"Yes, this training was not easy and had many consequences for the base of the 'Eagle'. But in the end, everything will be fine, we just have to be patient," said Nicholas Henderson, smiling discreetly. "At least it will work for those who believe."

"So, let's get started," Jennifer Henderson said, looking at everyone in the room. "After the android Marines announced a bounty for couples' wedding rings, our struggle has increased even more, and not to mention that we have a city of the 'Lost', very close to our base. And now they also try to attack us constantly..."

"And to make matters worse, it seems that the 'Lost' were trying to bring living beings negatively affected by the bioweapon to attack us and thus take advantage of the situation," adds Nicholas Henderson, gesturing with his hands. "But things got out of hand and the monsters escaped from the big cage and attacked everyone in the city, including our 'ALLIANCE WARRIORS'."

"And what were these couples doing in the city of the 'Lost'," Mr. Henderson? Emma Thompson asks nervously and punching the table. "I apologize to everyone for my attitude," she calmly removes her hands from the table. "We should never let emotion act before reason."

"I believe everyone here understands your concern, Emma. But answering your question, these couples were infiltrated into the city of the “Lost” as spies; they were the ones who brought us the information about the place. And with our infiltrated spies, we discover that the “Lost” have allied themselves with both types of androids. At least, that's the information our spies passed on."

"And according to the latest data collected, you passed through the city shortly after the attack of the negatively contaminated living beings ended," adds Jennifer Henderson.

"That's why the city was all erased and abandoned," William Thompson deduces thoughtfully. "Tell us more, Mr. Henderson, we want more details of what happened."

"In fact, the city is not totally abandoned. Supposedly, in this city of the “Lost”, people use underground hideouts to escape any kind of attack; And it seems that as soon as the animals escaped from the cage, people ran for cover or at least those who managed to run."

Jennifer, with a worried face, looks at her husband and says:

"But the worst is yet to come, now, those beasts that the 'Lost' let escape from the cage, are on the loose and seem to have human taste. We have not been able to see these monsters in person, but we do have information that these beasts are roaming our base and could attack at any time."

"We also need to help the people who are in the city of the 'Lost', because regardless of the circumstances, we are all human," said Nicholas Henderson, worried. "And we can find spies of ours there."

"We have to eliminate these beasts before they claim more victims," says Jennifer Henderson, holding her husband's hand. "It seems that these beasts have made the city and around it their territory."

"So we need to do something as soon as possible," says William Thompson.

"Tomorrow morning, one team will go to the city of the 'Lost' to rescue the survivors, and another team will try to locate the beasts in probable caves near the city, as we will have the advantage of ending these things in daylight," explains Nicholas Henderson.

"You can count on us in this fight!" William Thompson says to get up from the table. "We will only follow our destiny when we solve this problem of the 'Swallow' base.

Nicholas gets up from the table, hugs William, and says:

"I appreciate your help, as we will need all the help

we have available to resolve this situation. So you all rest tonight, and tomorrow we will meet at the refueling and training station."

Liam, Anne, Noah, Sophia, William and Emma say goodbye to the elderly couple Nicholas and Jennifer and leave the meeting room.

# INTENSIVE TRAINING

Early in the morning, Liam Cooper, Anne Smith, Noah Cooper, Sophia Johnson, William Thompson, and Emma Thompson are already in the refueling and training area of the "Swallow" base. On-site, there are a few couples of tables and chairs, where couples line up to insert their hands that wear the rings together into devices that sit on top of the tables. The devices show a 3D image that shows that the power of these alliances has been fully restored. On site, there were also training booths that couples entered and left together, these places had queues to be used. There were also screens that showed the training of the couples. Both the tables and the training booths were divided into three groups, and each group had a very visible notice (ring training and retrieval sector for couples/ring training and retrieval sector for newlyweds/bracelet training and retrieval sector for recruits). The recruitment sector is the only area that does not have couples, just a training booth with the light on, showing that it is occupied.

"I see that the couples here at the base of the 'Swallow' also start training very early," comments William Thompson, observing the place.

A couple finishes charging the energy of their rings and walks towards the training area.

"We're ready for another hard workout, my love," the husband said, hugging his wife.

"If we keep training like this, together we will be unbeatable," said the wife, smiling and looking into her husband's eyes.

The couple arrived in line, where there were other

couples waiting to train. The door to the training cabin opens, and one couple leaves and another couple enters. The couple who left the training cabin head towards the energy recovery site of the rings.

"It was great training, love," said the happy wife. "I'm very proud of you."

"I was only able to succeed in the training because you were there, my love," the husband said, lifting his wife in the air and spinning her around. "Let's charge up the energy of our wedding rings and come back for another workout and become even stronger together," he stopped his wife on the floor and kissed.

The couple hugs and walks to the line where there are other couples waiting to charge the energy of their rings.

"Attention!" commands Emma Thompson pointing to one of the screens where some couples faced ninjas and marines in a forest. "Look at that training where the couples are facing the android ninjas and the android marines in the same combat."

William and the four recruits look in the direction of the screens broadcasting the training and see couples struggling with all their might to survive in a forest, while the husbands attacked and defended themselves from their opponents with their short and long range weapons, the wives helped their husbands with their available resources.

"These simulators in the training booths are very real," says Sophia, admiring the couples' training.

"This training area is identical to our base, as the training ranges here are also interconnected and have training options for individual or group couples," says Noah Cooper, impressed by the location. "This is all very cool."

"Not only that, but the training booths here also have the option to train couples against couples," explains Anne Smith, gesturing with one hand and pointing to the entire training area. "This is a small but updated base."

"This is amazing!" Sophia Johnson said with great enthusiasm. "May the best couple win!"

"And where is the couples' training partner exchange area?" Noah Cooper asks, looking at Anne and Liam. "Then you two make the training partner switch."

Anne and Liam exchange glances without answering Noah's question. Until Sophia interrupts them both.

"Is everything okay with you two?" Sophia Johnson asks, running her hand in front of Liam and Anne's eyes. "Guys, Noah and I asked you a question."

Anne and Liam wake up, stop looking at each other, and Anne replies:

"Yes, it's okay. The place is right there."

Anne points to an area where there were a few separate individual tables and chairs; This place had the tables in different positions from the alliance recovery table.

"After all, is everything okay with you two?" Noah Cooper asks, finding the situation strange. "You two are always fighting, but it seems like one can't live without the other."

"It's okay with me," Liam Cooper replies, convinced of what he's saying. "I can't wait to resolve this situation with Anne and then be able to go on my way."

Anne, with a serious face and looking at Liam, asks:

"And you think I didn't think of that, Liam? But there is no couple available to make the switch at the moment."

Liam looks at Anne, and then the two look at Sophia

and Noah.

"Don't even think about it!" Noah Cooper said, shaking his head. "You two, forget about that possibility!"

"You two, don't bring your problems to both of us," Sophia Johnson said, holding Noah's hand. "Noah and I already have our own battles to worry about."

"That's right, me and Sophia will be together until death do us part," says Noah Cooper hugging Sophia.

"I was sure you two wouldn't accept it," said Anne Smith, despondent. "If I were with David, I wouldn't want to trade teammates with anyone either."

Liam finishes listening to what Anne said, sounds serious, and then says:

"Then we can try with the two recruits who stayed here at the base. It may be that they have not gone to the "Macaw" base because the two must not be understanding each other either."

"It doesn't hurt to try," Anne agrees, looking at Liam with a hostile face.

William sees the elderly couple, Mr. Nicholas and Mrs. Jennifer, on the scene and giving the last instructions to a group of couples, William communicates with his wife and the four recruits:

"There's the old couple, let's go to them."

William, Emma, and the two recruited couples walk towards the elderly couple. Nicholas and his wife, Jennifer, spot William and the others coming towards them, dismiss the couples who were being instructed, and begin walking towards William, Emma, and the others.

"Again, I say. It is an honor to welcome you all here to my small base, "Swallow," said Mr. Nicholas Henderson, greeting everyone.

"And once again I say... We are the ones who are grateful for the accommodation," William Thompson said jokingly. "And how are the plans for today, Mr. Henderson?"

"I've already sent a group of tracking couples to try to find the beasts and another group of rescue couples to rescue the 'Lost' and the spy couples to bring them here until all of this is resolved. And I have plans for us today, but first, I wanted to know."

Nicholas puts his hands on William's shoulder and asks:

"How was breakfast? I hope you enjoyed it, because I don't like my guests to be unhappy with the reception."

"It was delicious, I wouldn't change anything that was served this morning," said Liam Cooper, running his hand over his own belly, showing that he is satisfied.

Anne and Noah put their hands on their faces, showing disapproval of Liam's attitude.

"Everyone knows you don't have good manners, Liam Cooper, you don't need to keep drawing attention to yourself," said Anne Smith indignantly. "Don't you know that when the elders are talking, you can't interrupt?"

"Anne is right, brother," Noah Cooper agrees.

"I just told the truth," says Liam Cooper, downplaying the situation.

Jennifer interrupts the recruits' conversation and speaks:

"I am very happy to know that you all liked it, because my other cooks did everything with a lot of love and affection."

"My wife and I wanted you all to know the recruit

couple who didn't go to train at the 'Macaw" base," Nicholas Henderson said enthusiastically.

"You just have to wait a little longer, because the two recruits are still finishing their duties," warns Jennifer Henderson.

Liam looks around, looking for the recruit couple, and asks:

"Where is this couple that I'm not seeing?"

Jennifer and her husband look in the direction of the recruits' training booths. Anne grabs Liam's head and spins it in the direction of the training booths and asks:

"Have you forgotten that they're the only recruits here and that the recruits' training booth is on, Liam Cooper?"

"I still don't understand?"

Anne puts her hand on her face, shakes her head negatively, and says:

"I give up trying to explain the obvious to you, Liam."

"Anne, do you know these recruits they're talking about?" Noah Cooper asks.

"No, on this 'Swallow' base, I only know the old couple, because I wasn't much of a fan of leaving the main base until it was taken over by the androids."

And after a few seconds, the recruits' training booth opens the door and the couple of recruits, Adam Scott and Elizabeth White, come out of the training booth, he is a 17-year-old white young man, thin with curly red hair; She, on the other hand, is a 17-year-old white girl, thin and with curly blonde hair. Nicholas and Jennifer begin to gesture with their hands to get the attention of the recruit couple.

Jennifer shouts:

"Adam!" Elizabeth! We are here!

"Come here, you two!" Nicholas Henderson is still gesturing with his hands. "We want you to meet some recruits."

The recruit couple sees the elderly couple, starts smiling, holds hands, and walks towards them. Liam puts his hand on the back of his head, looks at Anne laughing when he sees the recruit couple, and says:

"Now I understand, Anne, when you spoke of the training booth."

"How inattentive you are, Liam," says Anne Smith, putting her hand on her face and making a negative sign. "Now, Liam, keep quiet and let's understand why the two recruits didn't go to the training at the “Macaw” base, and if we can still make the exchange with them."

"Okay, I get it, Anne," Liam Cooper says, rubbing one hand over the other. "We will analyze and then act."

Sophia discreetly comments in a low voice to Liam, Anne, and Noah:

"That's why the couple should work out their problems together. Because most of the time, there are a lot of people outside of the relationship rooting for the couple to break up instead of rooting for the couple to stay together."

"And as we've heard before, the best way for a couple to stay connected all the time is through dialogue," explains Noah Cooper, looking into Sophia's eyes. "Dialogue increases the connection between the couple and closes the gaps for the enemy."

"The dialogue between the couple is a fatal weapon for any suspicious threat," adds Sophia Johnson, returning

Noah's gaze.

Anne and Liam look at Noah and Sophia with faces of astonishment.

"You don't have to talk about it now, for I feel like a monster now," said Anne Smith with a sad countenance. "But I agree with everything you two said," she gets excited again.

"I also don't change a word of what has been said at this point," says Liam Cooper, gesturing with his hands. "But since Anne and I are not matching and we are about to kill each other..."

Anne interrupts Liam and concludes:

"What Liam means is that the recruit couple who stayed here at the base may be having some difficulty and may be looking for someone to make the switch as well. And I'm going to make it very clear that I already have my training partner and I just need to get to him."

"And I'm just giving myself one more chance and trying to find someone special to live with me for the rest of my life," Liam says mockingly. "What happened to me in that training session is in the past."

"Brother, if I didn't know you, I'd say only part of what you said is true," Noah Cooper said suspiciously of Liam. "But I still want to believe in you."

"What are you planning, Liam?" Sophia Johnson asks, also suspicious. "Tell us."

"I'm not planning anything," Liam Cooper replies, becoming a little disoriented and gesturing with his arms. "It's the plain truth what I just said."

"We understand, brother, there is no need to keep explaining yourself."

"Everyone pay attention," Sophia Johnson said, speaking softly. "I didn't want to say anything, but this couple that is coming, for the emotion that came out of the training, for the smile of the two, and for the holding hands. Everything indicates that they have a great connection. Their problem must be anything but disagreement between them."

Liam asks for silence with his finger and warns:

"So let's find out now what the problem is with the two of them, because they just arrived."

The recruit couple, Adam and Elizabeth, walk towards the elderly couple and the others. Nicholas introduces the recruit couple from the “Macaw” base:

"This young couple is Adam Scott and Elizabeth White. Adam Scott and Elizabeth White are the recruits, Liam Cooper, Anne Smith, Noah Cooper, Sophia Johnson, and their leaders, Mr. William Thompson and Mrs. Emma Thompson."

Everyone greets each other with hand gestures. Jennifer approaches Adam and Elizabeth from behind and says:

"How was the training of the two of you today?"

"We had a great result," replies Adam Scott enthusiastically. "But I still have the same problems as always," he comments sadly.

Elizabeth holds Adam's hand tightly and tries to lift his spirits:

"Even though Adam doesn't have combat weapon skills, he's very skilled with his own body. I felt totally protected by him."

Adam shakes Elizabeth's hand affectionately and cracks a smile. Nicholas begins to explain:

"As I mentioned before, this is a couple of recruits who did not go to the training at the "Macaw" base together with the other recruits, because they are facing difficulty with combat weapons. Adam can't really handle ranged weapons or close-range weapons in combat, but he excels at hand-to-hand combat with his own body. He uses punches, kicks, and submissions very effectively."

Liam jokes about the situation:

"And you still want to give this kid a combat weapon?"

Adam laughs a little and then explains:

"What you said was funny. But I manage to do all these feats thanks to my future wife, who already knows me and is always helping me."

"I can only do my part very successfully because you make things easier for me by helping me, you are the love of my life," says Elizabeth White, holding her partner's hand.

Elizabeth and Adam exchange glances and smiles, and Anne comments in a low voice:

"Abort the swap mission, Liam.

"You don't have to say it twice, Anne. I'm already realizing that it's another couple who have the same connection as Sophia and my brother."

"If the couple has a positive connection, the enemy runs away before they even try anything against the couple," Sophia Johnson said calmly and jokingly about the situation.

Nicholas gestures with his hands and speaks:

"Now that we have all been properly introduced. I wanted to talk about today's schedule. Today we will have a training for the six recruits."

"This would be a great opportunity for recruits to

hone their combat skills," William Thompson says enthusiastically.

"This training can be very good for you, Adam," Jennifer Henderson said, encouraging the recruit. "That way, you might end up acquiring some skill with combat weapons."

"That would be amazing!" Adam Scott agrees, clenching his fists and perking up.

"And for starters, all recruits are free to go to the bracelet loading area and the resource and weapon store to see what's available," Emma Thompson says enthusiastically.

"And for the training with the bracelets, I will take it upon myself to increase their capacity so that all of you have more options for resources and skills in combat," said Mr. Nicholas Henderson enthusiastically. "When everyone is ready, you go to the training area for new recruits."

"Now, this subject of training for new recruits is getting more interesting," Noah Cooper said, clenching his fists. "That way, Sophia and I can increase our connection and become even stronger.

"So, let's all get ready!" William Thompson orders, raising his hand. "We still have a long way to go."

"Honey, let's recharge our wristbands and get ready for training," Adam Scott said, punching the wind as if he were training. "I believe that this training can do a lot of good for our relationship."

"You can count on me, honey," says Elizabeth White, smiling at her workout partner.

Liam speaks softly to Anne after seeing how Adam and Elizabeth had a great connection:

"Anne, I'm glad we didn't say anything about the exchange with the two recruits."

"And this matter had better stay between us, Liam. We don't want the recruit couple to have a bad impression of us."

"It's true. We don't want the two of them to have a bad impression of us, like my brother and Sophia did."

Sophia and Noah start laughing softly after hearing Liam and Anne. Then everyone goes to the designated places.

# BROTHER AGAINST BROTHER

Liam Cooper, Anne Smith, Noah Cooper, Sophia Johnson, William Thompson, Emma Thompson, Nicholas Henderson, Jennifer Henderson, Adam Scott, and Elizabeth White are gathered in the training area of the recruit couples. Nicholas looks at the recruited couples and says:

"Now that all the recruits are ready, we can start training. Their bracelets are already enabled at a higher level than before, and I hope everyone has wisely chosen their resources and weapons."

"As soon as you enter the training booths, they already have the training standard set," explains Ms. Jennifer Henderson, pointing to the training booths. "Remember, this is a workout, but it can happen in reality, so do your best."

"Recruits, fight in this training as if you were fighting for your own survival," advises William Thompson.

"And don't forget, this is not an individual fight, but in pairs, as a couple has to do," warns Emma Thompson, gesturing with her hands. "If couples are not united, they will easily lose to life's obstacles."

Noah holds his training partner's hands, looks her in the eye, and says:

"Sophia Johnson, I don't promise you the world, but what we achieve is first for you and then for me. You are my priority."

Sophia looks into the eyes of her training partner and says:

"And you're my priority, Noah Cooper. And I was sure of that, from the day you not only proved with words, but with attitudes, that you were a great companion."

"Look at this, Elizabeth," Adam Scott said, looking at Sophia and Noah. "We will have a strong couple in this training to compete with us."

"Adam, dear, I realized this from the moment I saw the two of them."

"You women have a higher level of attention than we men," Adam says, impressed.

Elizabeth smiles, then looks in the direction of Liam and Anne and, realizing that the two have no connection, asks:

"And you two, do you have any purpose? Because I realized that the connection between the two of you is zero."

"Yes, Anne and I will complete today's training team as we don't have much to add," says Liam Cooper.

"That's not what I was referring to. I'm asking if you two have any goals in life?

"Now I understand what you want to know. I have a goal, but it is not with her."

Liam and Anne look at each other with contempt.

"I have my purpose together with my true partner, but there was a mistake in the 'Eagle' base, and we ended up changing training partners," said Anne Smith, still ignoring Liam.

"Yes, you two are the couple that doesn't match. We are already aware of this situation," Adam Scott said.

Liam grumbles in a low voice:

"I just realized that in this place there are gossips who like to talk about other people's lives."

"Did you say anything, Liam?"

"No, my friend, Adam, I'm just thinking out loud."

Elizabeth takes Anne's hands with great enthusiasm

and speaks:

"Anne, are you also from the 'Swallow' base? I heard that you are from the main base and that your parents are trying to get you back from the androids along with the "ALLIANCE WARRIORS" from the "Eagle" base."

"But this place is complicated, everyone knows each other's lives," Liam grumbles under his breath again. "And before anyone asks, I'm just thinking out loud," Liam warns when he realizes that everyone is looking at him.

Anne clenches her fists confidently and speaks:

"I just need to join my partner, David, and together we will dedicate ourselves to training to become 'ALLIANCE WARRIORS' and be able to help our parents reclaim our home."

"I like that attitude of yours, Anne," Nicholas Henderson said proudly. "That's what we expect from future couples, a lot of attitude," he clenches his fists. "Now, let's start with training. Couples can choose one of the training cabins and snuggle up. Even if one of the pairs does not start training in this first stage, just watch the other pairs fight and wait for their turn to train."

Each recruit couple enters a training booth. Inside the cabin were two seats and one more door. As soon as the recruits sit in the seats, a 3D image appears with a few options.

"Sophia, here on the screen shows that we are the first to train," says Noah Cooper, analyzing the options in the image.

"Yes, and this training is couple against couple, and our opponents are your brother and Anne."

"The location of the fight has also been defined,

Sophia."

"It's time to go to training, Noah."

"Let's see what will happen."

Noah and Sophia get up from their seats and enter through the other door, This door gives access to a Roman arena. Liam and Anne were still in their cabin seats, reviewing the available options.

"We're going to start facing my brother and Sophia," warns Liam Cooper, not liking what he's seeing at all. "That doesn't seem very fair to me, since they fight as a couple and I fight alone."

"Stop complaining and let's finish this training as soon as possible," Anne Smith said impatiently. "Liam, if you did your part, I wouldn't have a hard time doing mine."

"Anne, if you can at least equip me for combat, I believe I can beat my brother and Sophia."

"I'm going to make sure I equip you to see if you can really do anything in combat, Liam," says Anne Smith, dismissing the situation. "But I don't think you can go too far as you say."

"Look and watch the massacre against my brother," said Liam Cooper, starting to perk up in training. "My brother's long-range weapon doesn't stand a chance against my short-range weapon. Anne, equip me with resistance, that's your only mission," he says, belittling his partner.

"You don't have to keep telling me what to do, Liam, I know my obligations," Anne Smith said, losing her temper. "You don't have to worry because I already know what to do."

Liam and Anne enter the arena and come across Noah and Sophia on the other side of the arena. Noah jokes with his brother and Anne:

"I thought you two had given up training when you saw who your opponents were."

"Stop dreaming, my brother, I'm going to defeat you two by myself," Liam Cooper said confidently. "You'll need much more than a medieval beast to defeat me." Get ready to take on the great Liam Cooper."

"Then that's how you think you can act," Anne said in a low, indignant voice to Liam. "Let's see if you can do something without me."

An artificial voice of a woman infiltrates the place:

"Start training!"

Anne, Liam, Sophia, and Noah activate their energetic protections. Liam activates his sword, raises it with both hands, starts running with all his speed towards Noah, and shouts:

"I'm sorry, brother!" But here will be the end of that workout for you!

William, Emma, Nicholas, and Jennifer watch the fight on the big screen in the training area.

"That doesn't look good at all," comments Emma Thompson, not liking what she is seeing.

"As the saying goes, 'It is by falling that one learns,'" William Thompson said, running his hand over his head.

Adam and Elizabeth watch the combat through the screen in the training cabin. He comments:

"I don't know how Liam and Anne got here with this individualistic style of combat."

"They're both in the wrong place if they think about fighting individually," said Elizabeth White.

Back at the training arena, Sophia analyzes Liam in

her 3D image. The analysis shows that Liam is already running out of energy in his bracelet, and she speaks in a low voice:

"I won't have to do much for what I'm seeing."

Sophia accesses the options of her features in 3D, selects the protection boost for Noah, and her bracelets start to glow. Noah activates his crossbow and aims it at Liam, but gives up firing the arrow when he realizes that his brother is already exhausted. He comments:

"If my brother keeps thinking that he solves everything by himself, he won't get very far in this life."

Liam stops running, and his sword begins to fail. Liam's sword begins to activate and deactivate in his hand. Liam arrives tired near Noah, but when he tries to strike a blow with the sword, the sword is completely deactivated. Liam looks at Anne, who shows no concern for the situation. Anne is looking and fiddling with her nails, and Liam, incredulous, says:

"I can't believe this crazy Anne won't do anything to help me."

"It's over, brother!" Noah Cooper screams.

Liam looks at his brother again and sees his brother's fist coming towards him. Noah punches Liam, who knocks him out of the arena. Liam and Anne return to their seats in the training cabin with a teleportation, and they both begin to argue.

"I lost because of you, Anne Smith! You didn't trigger the stamina skill on me like I asked!"

"First of all, you don't boss me around! Secondly, you said you would win the fight against your brother and Sophia alone! So I deduced that you wouldn't need my help, Liam

Cooper."

Liam threatens to speak, but gives up speaking, and Anne continues:

"So next time, see if you don't try to work things out your way and on your own. And let this serve as a lesson for you, Liam."

"I can't wait to change training partners," Liam Cooper said in a calmer, more despondent tone of voice. "You and I don't agree on anything, Anne."

"I think the same thing as you, Liam."

Liam and Anne cross their arms and stop talking, meanwhile, Sophia and Noah run to hug each other, and they begin to celebrate the victory together.

"I don't even know why we're celebrating?" Noah Cooper asks cheerfully. "This fight against my brother and Anne was easy for us."

"We have to celebrate life's small and big achievements," replies Sophia Johnson cheerfully. "But more than celebrating, we have to know how to be grateful at all times, whether in the easy or difficult ones, whether in small or large achievements. Always be grateful."

"And once again, I'm sure I'm with the right person to spend the rest of my life with," says Noah Cooper, proud and looking into Sophia's eyes.

Noah and Sophia hug again and are teleported to the training cabin. Sophia observes the screen and speaks:

"It looks like the next training session is about to start, Noah."

"Let's get ready, Sophia, because we can be ourselves again. Since there are only three couples participating in the training."

"Look, Noah!" It is his brother and Anne against Adam and Elizabeth."

"I hope my brother and Anne have learned something after this last training against both of us, Sophia."

Sophia nods in agreement with Noah and says:

"I hope so, but your brother has become a difficult person to deal with."

"I know this, but I insist, my brother wasn't always like this," Noah Cooper agrees with a sad look. "Liam just has to move on and get over what happened to him in the past.

Sophia holds Noah's hand."

# AN INTERRUPTED TRAINING

The next fight is about to begin. Elizabeth White and Adam Scott look at each other, smile, give a thumbs-up, and enter the arena. The training arena this time is a large rock in the middle of a canyon. Adam looks around, analyzing the place, and comments:

"Elizabeth, my dear. In this training, there are two ways to win."

"Yes, I realized when analyzing the place where we are going to fight, my love. Either we deplete Anne's energy, or we throw one of the two off the rock."

Liam Cooper and Anne Smith, both discouraged, realize that they are the chosen ones for the next practice.

"I didn't even have time to absorb the last defeat," comments Liam Cooper, frustrated.

"Let's finish this as soon as possible, Liam, because I don't see any advantage in this training as we are both an absolute mistake," said Anne Smith, handing over the points.

"I have to agree with you, Anne, this training doesn't make sense for both of us. In fact, it doesn't make sense for both of us to continue training until we resolve our situation."

Liam and Anne enter the combat arena, both still despondent. Elizabeth and Adam look at their opponents and see that they have no interest in training. Adam looks at Elizabeth, and she gives a thumbs up. Adam gestures with one hand to get his opponents' attention and then tries to encourage them:

"Liam and Anne! Look at this training as if it were in reality, if the two of you don't face the challenges together, the challenges will face both of you. Now I'm speaking as a friend, But once this training begins, my partner and I will be the challenge of the moment for both of you."

Liam and Anne look at each other for a moment, and Anne, still discouraged, speaks:

"Liam, I'm going to allow resistance on you, and you do what you think is best in this fight."

"See what you can do, Anne," said Liam Cooper, still showing no interest in the workout. "Anyway, in the end, I will have to do everything myself."

An artificial voice of a man infiltrates the place:

"Start training!"

Liam, Anne, Adam, and Elizabeth activate their energetic protections. Elizabeth selects a few options from her resources and speaks:

"Adam, I equipped you with endurance and strength. As much as this fight seems won for us and even though it's just a training session, we can't open a gap for the opponent."

Adam and Elizabeth's bracelets begin to glow. Adam gives a thumbs-up sign to his partner.

"How is it going to be, Liam and Anne? Are you both ready to lose to someone who doesn't even use combat weapons?" Adam Scott asks, taunting his opponents. "I believe that this attitude of mine can encourage you to train," he says in a low voice.

Liam looks at Anne, and she just moves her shoulder. Liam, showing discouragement, activates his sword and shield and prepares for combat. Anne, not caring much about the situation, chooses the resistance option in her resources and equips Liam. The bracelets of the two begin to glow with little intensity. Liam, seeing that he has been equipped with an ability, looks at Anne again, and this time she gives a thumbs up. Liam and Anne communicate through the bracelets.

"Liam, this time I did my part, now, see if you do yours."

"Don't worry about me, Anne, I know my obligations."

In the training booth, Noah and Sophia watch the training on the screen. He comments:

"This is still not good. They are doing things anyway and out of obligation."

"Even if both of you fulfill your duties individually, it doesn't mean that you will succeed in training or in life's challenges," Sophia Johnson explains with a negative nod. "As long as they don't understand that it has to be for each other, everything becomes more difficult."

On the training rock, Adam sees that Liam is ready to start training. He gets into a fighting position and taunts him once again:

"I noticed that you got a little excited for this fight, Liam. But that won't be enough to defeat me. I expected more from those who know how to handle a close-range weapon with this medieval sword."

"Adam, you talk too much!" Liam Cooper said in a serious tone of voice. "Now you're starting to make me angry. You won't be as lucky as my brother," he with his sword and shield activated, gets into a fighting stance. "This time, I have something to show in combat."

"Then show me what you can do, Liam!" Adam Scott screams, starting to run towards his opponent.

"I'm going to show what I'm capable of," said Liam

Cooper, still in combat position.

Adam approaches Liam, jumps into the air, and attacks his opponent with a kick. Liam defends himself from the kick with his shield and goes on the counterattack with his sword. Liam performs several blows while Adam is on the defensive, dodging. Then Liam does a few somersaults and gets into a fighting position again, realizes that he was punched in the abdomen and, feeling pain, puts his hand on the spot and comments:

"How did I not see that punch?"

"I see you have a lot of skill with swords, but what you have in abundance in skills with close-range weapons reads a lack work in pairs," Adam Scott said entering combat stance. "You didn't notice, but my companion quickly traded stamina for agility and I punched you without you noticing at first," he winks at Elizabeth and she reciprocates the gesture.

"Anne, empower me with regeneration! I can still beat him," said Liam Cooper, looking at his training partner.

"I'm trying, but my resource options are blocked again," warns Anne Smith, unable to access her resources. "This is too bad," Anne's 3D image shows all the options with a warning written: “Lack of connection”. "Liam, I can't do anything from here because our connection is weak, so the bracelets cut our connection. And to make matters worse, the energy in your bracelet is also running out."

"What do I do now?" Liam Cooper asks without reaction.

"Liam!" Anne Smith screams, gesturing with her hands. "Try to attack him with the rest of the energy you have."

Liam raises his thumb and says:

"Finally, you've done something, Anne."

Anne is furious, starts gesturing with her hands again, and shouts:

"It's not my fault if you think you're always right, Liam Cooper. You think you're the best of all, but the truth is that you can't do anything alone!"

"I was kidding, there's no need to be nervous," said Liam Cooper, startled by Anne's attitude. "But now look and learn how to win a fight, Anne," he says with confidence.

"Liam, you like to drive people crazy," said Anne Smith, sulking and crossing her arms.

Liam smiles at Anne and then starts running towards Adam with his sword and the rest of his remaining energy. William and his wife watch combat from the training area. He comments:

"These two were definitely not made for each other."

"Let's let the future decide that, my love, as it's still too early to jump to conclusions," said Emma Thompson, observing the fight.

"But this fight is already more than defined, dear. Anyone can see the winner of this fight."

"Yes, but falls can encourage the couple to get up stronger and move forward with new learning. And it is up to the couple whether they will continue to suffer from the same mistake or if they have overcome the mistake."

On the rock, Liam approaches Adam and tries to hit him with his sword, holding it with both hands. But the power of his bracelet fails, and the sword is deactivated. Adam nods, grabs Liam, and throws him off the cliff, ending the training. Adam runs up to Elizabeth, lifts her up high, and hugs her. Both celebrate the victory.

"We both managed to win this battle, my love!" Elizabeth White said very happily and looking into her companion's eyes.

"And it's all thanks to your skill with resources, because if you weren't so good with it, I couldn't do anything, because I'm not able to fight with any kind of combat weapon," Adam Scott said proudly of his training partner.

"And yet, I think you're amazing, because you do the impossible with what you have to protect me. And I am a witness to this, no one needs to tell me about your courage."

Adam and Elizabeth hug tightly and are then teleported to the training cabin. Liam is still falling off the cliff and, dejected, says:

"It's not possible that I'm so wrong."

Liam hears Anne's voice coming from his bracelet:

"You still have the courage to say that you are not wrong."

Liam and Anne are also teleported to the training cabin again. The two begin to argue once again. Anne begins to imitate Liam mockingly:

"But now look and learn how to win a fight, Anne". Look at the size of the absurdity I have to hear from you, Liam."

"But the disaster of this fight was because of you, Anne," said Liam Cooper, frustrated. "If you did your part of the training correctly, none of this would have happened."

"My fault?! My fault?!" Anne Smith screams, clenching her fists and threatening to hit Liam. "You are the one who thinks that a problem where you depend on two people to solve it can be solved by just one person. You're a selfish, Liam! She lowers her hands, giving up on assaulting Liam."

"I don't know why you're so upset, I'm the one who has to do it all myself. You just gave an idea at the end of the training session, and you are already feeling like the best person in the world."

Anne gets angry again and furious, she says:

"I don't really know why I was trying to help you, even though everything was going wrong, Liam, because you don't deserve my help. Do you know why? Because you think there are only your problems in the world and no one else's. And look what happened, we lost again. Liam Cooper, you're very arrogant. Because if there was no way to activate the features, it's because you don't do your part right either! You don't collaborate!"

"Anne, I'm not going to stay here arguing with you, it's not worth it."

"At least own up to your mistakes, be a man, Liam!"

"Look at the screen, Anne, because the next training session is about to start. Pay attention to see if you learn anything."

"You don't boss me around."

"And you say I'm the only one who's selfish and arrogant here."

"Shut up, Liam."

Noah and Sophia watch Anne and Liam's argument on the screen. Noah comments:

"These two will never understand each other if they continue to act like this."

"They look like cats and dogs when they're at war," Sophia Johnson said, drawing a comparison.

Adam and Elizabeth also watch from the screen, Liam and Anne argue. Adam comments:

"I've never seen a couple disagree so much. Because when the couple sees that it won't work out, they have already changed at the beginning."

"From what I understand, Liam and Anne didn't change because the system of the 'Eagle' base failed. And both were very unlucky because the system brought them together," explains Elizabeth White.

"Look, Elizabeth! We're the ones who are going to train now," said Adam Scott, pointing his finger at the screen.

"Yes! It's the two of us against Noah and Sophia. These two won't be as easy as Liam and Anne."

"You're absolutely right, just like the two of us, they also have a great connection."

Adam and Elizabeth enter the arena, where they meet Noah and Sophia. This is an ice arena, and the two couples are already getting ready to start the fight. They activate their energetic protection.

"Sophia, I think we've found a matching opponent," Noah Cooper said, communicating through his bracelet. "We will have to fight more united than before."

"I'm with you, Noah," Sophia Johnson said excitedly through her bracelet. "In joy and in sadness, right?"

"Okay, Sophia, together we are unbeatable."

From the training booth, Liam and Anne observe everything that is happening in the training arena. Liam grumbles:

"In addition to everything I'm going through, I still haven't heard my brother say that I'm not a worthy opponent.

"And I see these two couples having a great

connection," Anne Smith said cheerfully. "It reminds me of me and David together."

"How dramatic you are, Anne."

"Look who's talking. “On top of everything I'm going through, I still haven't heard my brother say that I'm not a worthy opponent," Anne Smith said mockingly and imitating Liam.

"You're serious, are you going to imitate me all the time now?" And I don't talk like that, the way you're imitating me," complains Liam Cooper, in a bad mood.

"You're always making me angry, Liam!"

"And you're not the easiest person to deal with on this planet," Liam Cooper said mockingly.

"Let's see your brother and Sophia fight my countrymen," Anne Smith said, putting her hand in front of Liam's mouth. "I can't stand to hear your voice anymore, Liam."

In the training area, William, Emma, Nicholas, and Jennifer also observe everything that is happening.

"It looks like we're now going to have a battle with two high-status couples," comments Mr. Nicholas Henderson enthusiastically.

"This is a good sign, because in this way, the two couples can increase their connections and Liam and Anne can learn something from this training," said Emma Thompson, looking at Liam and Anne through the screen.

"I wanted to comment, Elizabeth and Adam will face the strongest recruit couple at the “Eagle” base," William Thompson said proudly.

"This is going to be amazing, since Elizabeth and Adam are amazing together, because what Adam lacks in skill with combat weapons, Elizabeth has skill to spare with resource options," said Mrs. Jennifer Henderson, clapping and very happy.

"This fight is going to be very interesting," Nicholas Henderson said, rubbing one hand over the other.

"Attention! The fight is about to begin," warns Emma Thompson.

In the training arena, an artificial voice of a woman infiltrates the place:

"Start training!"

And when Sophia and Elizabeth activate their feature options, Adam gets into combat stance, and Noah activates his crossbow and points an arrow in Adam's direction. An alarm starts ringing all over the "Swallow" base, and the woman's artificial voice says again:

"Training canceled! Training canceled!"

Noah, Sophia, Adam, and Elizabeth are teleported to their training cabins. Noah, Sophia, Adam, Elizabeth, Liam, and Anne, leave the cabins and join William, Emma, Nicholas and Jennifer in the training area.

"What's going on?" Noah asks, seeing men and women who were training running in the same direction.

"Why was the training stopped?" Elizabeth White asks without understanding anything.

"We still don't know the reason for this emergency," replies Mr. Nicholas Henderson.

"But we'll find out soon," says Ms. Jennifer Henderson.

Liam says in a low voice:

"The system could have canceled the training before I went through all that embarrassment in the last two training sessions."

"Stop complaining, Liam, we both deserve to go through all this we've been through," Anne Smith admits realistically. "As we only work individually, there would be no way to obtain any other result."

"And I don't remember asking your opinion, Anne."

"But someone has to warn you that you're not the center of attention in this world, Liam."

A couple of “ALLIANCE WARRIORS” approach the elderly couple.

"Mr. Henderson and Mrs. Henderson. The “Lost” and our spies have been found and are already at the base," says the husband.

"This is very good news!" said Mr. Nicholas Henderson, rejoicing. "But what is the reason for the alarm?" He asks suspiciously.

"The Lost” are receiving all the necessary care. But the “ALLIANCE WARRIORS” are having trouble regaining the energy of their wedding rings," replies the discouraged wife.

William, Emma, Nicholas, and Jennifer look at each other with looks of disappointment. Mr. Henderson orders:

"Let's all go to the recovery area of the “ALLIANCE WARRIORS” alliance.

"All of this smells very bad," comments Anne Smith, observing the situation.

"You just need to take a shower, Anne."

Anne takes Liam's arm and, with a straight face, says softly:

"Liam, stop trying to get attention. You look like a spoiled child. You haven't realized that something serious is happening here at the base."

As Anne and Liam argue, Noah walks up to Adam, takes his hand, and says:

"It was going to be a big fight between the four of us, Adam."

"I'm sure of it, Noah. But there will be no shortage of opportunities for the four of us to train.

Elizabeth approaches Sophia and says jokingly:

"We won't be as easy to defeat as Liam and Anne."

"I was going to say the same thing as you, Elizabeth," Sophia Johnson said with a laugh.

"I'm going to keep quiet at this point so I don't have any more problems with anyone," says Liam Cooper indignantly after listening to Elizabeth and Sophia.

"That's the best thing you do, Liam," Anne Smith agrees impatiently.

Liam, Anne, Noah, Sophia, William, Emma, Nicholas, Jennifer, Adam, and Elizabeth go to the recovery area.

# BETRAYAL IS A CHOICE AND NOT WEAKNESS

Liam Cooper, Anne Smith, Noah Cooper, Sophia Johnson, William Thompson, Emma Thompson, Nicholas Henderson, Jennifer Henderson, Adam Scott, and Elizabeth White arrive at the alliance's recovery area. The place has many couples. Jennifer opens a 3D image with the energy of her wedding ring and realizes that there is something wrong with the statuses of some couples and that these same couples are having a hard time carrying the energy of their wedding rings. Ms. Jennifer, with a straight face, comments:

"Of the spy couples who were sent to the city of the 'Lost', some of them returned with a very low rating."

"That's weird, because we send the couples with the highest levels and the highest ratings," said Nicholas Henderson, dissatisfied. "And if the rating has dropped, that's a sign that the connection between these couples has diminished for some reason."

Liam nudges his brother and asks in a low voice:

"Doesn't the level of a couple of 'ALLIANCE WARRIORS' decrease because of the length of the marriage? But does the ranking constantly change depending on the couple's connection?"

"That's right, my brother," Noah Cooper replies quietly. "I see that you still know the rules of the 'ALLIANCE WARRIORS' couples.

"I asked so that there were no doubts in my head. Therefore, it is better to ask than not to learn."

Then, a couple of "ALLIANCE WARRIORS" arrive at the elderly couple.

"Mr. and Mrs. Henderson," said the distressed husband. "We are having serious problems with a couple of spies who have returned from the city of the 'Lost', and the situation tends to worsen."

"Take a deep breath, my friend, are you two also one of the spy couples who were sent to the city of the 'Lost'? Nicholas Henderson asks, trying to stay calm. "Tell us what you two know about this situation!"

"Sir, it seems that we have spent a lot of time in the city of the "Lost", replies the wife trying to calm her husband. And many husbands and wives, many married couples, did not resist "till death do us part". If you know what I mean?"

Jennifer, with a serious and sad face at the same time, looks at the couple of spies and asks:

"In total, how many couples will fall into dishonor? Have we had many losses?"

"Madam, the couples who have fallen are not even 15% of the total number of couples sent to the city of the "Lost"," replies the wife with sadness in her eyes and trembling voice. "But given the circumstances we face, I believe it will make all the difference in the future."

"It's really a considerable number, because every couple who falls into dishonor is not only condemning their partner, but themselves," agrees Mrs. Jennifer Henderson, incredulous and indignant. "I cannot understand how there can be people who do not respect those who declare "in health and in sickness, in joy and in sorrow"."

The wife nods in agreement with Jennifer. Nicholas looks at the couple and says with great pride:

"You are both to be congratulated, because from what I see, you have resisted the temptations of the world."

"The secret was me and my wife keeping the connection at all times, no matter how hard it seemed at times," explains the calmer husband, holding his wife's hand and looking into her eyes.

Husband and wife hug and exchange passionate glances.

"That's how it has to be between the couple; it can't be any other way," Nicholas Henderson said firmly in his tone of voice. "For a couple to win together, they need to always be connected with each other."

"There's something going on with some couples," warns Liam Cooper, not liking what he's seeing.

Anne, Noah, Sophia, William, Emma, Nicholas, Jennifer, Adam, Elizabeth, and a couple of spies begin to see couples crying and arguing. And some husbands and wives are dying after not recharging their wedding rings.

"How did you have the courage to betray me?" shouts one of the wives indignantly at her husband. "We were one. Have you forgotten what you promised me at the altar?"

The husband kneels on the floor, holds his wife's hand, begins to cry, and begs for forgiveness:

"Forgive me, my love! I made a mistake, and I regret it deeply, but it's you I love and want to spend the rest of my life with! Don't leave me, I beg you!"

"You are forgiven," his wife said, tears streaming down her face. "But we can't be together anymore," she says, letting go of her husband's hand. "The rule is very clear about marriage. I lost the trust I had in you."

"Don't do this to me!" asks the husband kissing his wife's feet. "I don't know how to live without you."

"Think about it before you do what you did," his wife

said in a firm tone of voice and wiping away her own tears. "I'll be filing for divorce. I won't carry the shame—you were the one who abandoned our vows. The weakness wasn't mine," she leaves, leaving her husband in tears.

"Don't do that, my love, please!" begs the husband, getting up from the floor, wiping the tears from his face, and running towards his future ex-wife. "Let's talk! I don't want to lose you!"

At the same moment, another couple was arguing and crying.

"I can't believe you did it, you irresponsible!" shouts the furious husband with tears in his eyes. "Since when did I stop being enough for you?"

"You never stopped being enough for me! But I was weak at that moment," admits his wife, crying and running her hands through her hair, desperate. "And I bitterly regret what I did. Forgive me! This will never be repeated."

"I can't forgive you! I can't even look you in the eye, you traitor!" shouts her husband, starting to hit himself. "How stupid I was to trust you," He anxiously toyed with his wedding ring.

"What are you going to do?" asks his wife in despair. "Don't do that!" She tries to hold her husband.

The husband pushes his wife, and she falls to the ground. The husband touches his wedding ring again and says:

"I don't see a reason to keep living."

"Please don't do that! We can try again. I made a mistake and now I know how important you are to me," begs his wife sitting on the floor.

The husband looks at his wife's face, both have tears

running down their faces, and he says calmly:

"I want to forgive him, but I don't have the strength to do so. I can't forgive you, I can't."

"Don't activate the self-destruction of the covenant, don't do that!" begs the wife, standing up and hugging her husband. "I made a mistake, but that doesn't mean I'm going to keep making the mistake."

"I can't forgive her, and I don't see the point in continuing to live," her husband said, causing his own destruction with the ring.

A blinding light consumed him, and he was pulverized, leaving only ashes. The wife falls to her knees on the floor and begins to cry, taking her ex-husband's ashes in her hands.

"I failed! I failed! I failed!" admits the wife, activating the high destruction of her wedding ring.

An energy of light takes over your body and is sprayed. Other couples begin to cry and argue. And some more wives and husbands do not forgive their partners and activate the high destruction of their marriage alliances. And once again, only the ashes of these people remain. Jennifer, with a downcast face and seeing the couples eliminating each other, says in a tone of sadness:

"The energy they use in the high destruction of wedding rings should not be used in this way, but rather in a last act of husband and wife in combat. In the case of wives, they release one last charge of skill energy; this energy is more enhanced than normal ones, and their husbands get a second chance at combat with the energy of their covenant charged and with more power. In the last act of the husbands, they throw an energy of protection on the wife and with that, she is thrown away from the battlefield, this attitude in combat is known as “sacrifice”, as it is to be used to leave the husband vulnerable and give a second chance to the wife."

William holds his wife's hand and, with a tone of sadness, explains:

"Many are seeing these deaths as if they were just carnal. But the truth is that this portrays a spiritual death as well. There is always someone who benefits from the separation of a couple, the end of a marriage, or the betrayal of someone. And the one who is benefiting is not always from this world, but also from the spiritual world."

"The person who betrays the one who swore 'till death do us part' does not know the harm he is bringing to his own life, to the life of his partner and to the life of his family, because his children may tread a dark path because of the irresponsibility of a traitor," explains Emma Thompson indignantly. "Betrayal can bring irreversible sequels in the life of a family, so I say that a marriage is not for everyone."

"Right now, the death rate is only growing," warns Mrs. Jennifer Henderson, analyzing the 3D image. "The number of husbands who die is three times greater than the number of wives."

"It may also indicate that the number of wives who forgive betrayal is greater than the number of husbands," Thompson said.

"You're correct," says Jennifer Henderson, still analyzing the situation. "Most wives are filing for divorce, but in the case of husbands, most of them cannot forgive and seek the destruction of their wedding rings, ending their own lives."

"Every betrayed husband or wife has a different reaction to the situation," says Anne Smith with teary eyes. "This is very sad.

"And most of the time, the betrayed end up killing their companions," explains William Thompson, discouraged. "And unfortunately, husbands are more likely to kill their partners."

"But as hard as it is, killing will never be the best option for a betrayal," said Emma Thompson, taking a deep breath. "The best thing is to seek your rights and distance yourself from the traitor."

The spy couple looks at the elderly couple, and the husband says:

"Mr. and Mrs. Henderson. We have stayed in the world for a long time. We spent too long in the city of the 'Lost', and many couples gave in to temptation.

"Betrayal can never be used as an excuse for a problem in the relationship," explains Mr. Nicholas Henderson, putting his hands behind his back. "Only people without character and weak use this as an alibi."

"In the city of the 'Lost', there were many temptations to the will of our body," explains the spy wife with a sad look. "And many couples did not resist and fell into the trap of the world."

Mrs. Jennifer takes the spy wife's hand and says:

"My young lady, I believe that you too have been tempted by many temptations of the world. Let me ask you a question. Have you and your husband fallen into a trap in the world?"

"No, ma'am," replies the spy wife in a firm voice.

"My husband and I keep our connection always active so as not to open a breach for the enemy."

Ms. Jennifer asks again:

"And do you know why you didn't fall into any trap in the world?"

"Yes, ma'am, I know the reason, because it was a matter of choice, ma'am," replies the spy wife in a stronger tone than before.

Mr. Nicolau, in a firm voice, explains:

"So, let it serve as a lesson for everyone. The world, or the enemy, as many like to call it, puts temptation in front of the person, but does not force him to enjoy sin. Only those who lack character throw away their relationship, sometimes of many years, for a few minutes of pleasure. Only the weak do this and still think they are champions. And who are often exalted by fools who may one day fall into their own trap."

"And many couples fall into the traps of the world because of their choices," adds Mrs. Jennifer Henderson with a straight face. "That's why, before you take on a relationship, remember to analyze your mates, as a weak partner can ruin your life forever."

"And the right companion can give you the strength to overcome any barrier in life," says Mr. Nicholas Henderson, raising his index finger. "It's not an easy journey, but it's not impossible either, because there are still couples who manage to go all the way together," he cracks a smile and points to some spy couples who have managed to overcome the temptations of the city of the "Lost" and the world.

"We managed to win together, my love," said the husband happily and hugging his wife.

"They tried to bring us down, but our connection was bigger than all the challenges we encountered along the way, honey," says the very cheerful wife, kissing her husband.

Husband and wife, still hugging, continue to walk together. Another couple also celebrates the victory.

"Many are those who want the destruction of the marriage, but the couple who are always in communication with each other will never betray their partner," said the husband, a little sadly. "I see that many couples have fallen and, unfortunately, there are husbands and wives who are not to blame for the failure of their partners."

"That's why you have to choose your partner for life carefully, because if only one makes an effort in the relationship, it's useless," adds the wife, holding her husband's hand. "We have no control over the attitude of the other. And if the companion falls into temptation, we can do nothing but gather what is left and move on."

"I'm very happy with the partner I've chosen to spend the rest of my life with," says her husband enthusiastically.

"“Until death do us part”," said the wife jokingly and hugging her husband. "And if we want our relationship to stay that way, we have to always be connected with each other."

The two walk, hugging and smiling at each other. Mr. Nicholas, with a hopeful look, speaks:

"Mr. William Thompson and Mrs. Emma Thompson, I ask you to prepare together with the recruits for the lunch that is about to be served. My wife and I are going to sort out some outstanding issues with the spy couple who have just arrived. Unfortunately, I have to settle some divorces and have a funeral for the dead, regardless of the circumstances.

As difficult as this whole situation is, we cannot stop because the enemy does not rest. And tonight, we'll be back with recruit training."

Mr. Nicholas looks at the six recruits and says:

"I hope you learned something today about betrayal. A person who betrays someone who one day promised to spend the rest of their life with, that person is a traitor to themselves."

The six recruits nod their heads in agreement. The elderly couple and the spy couple say goodbye to William, Emma, and the others. Then Emma calls the recruits' attention and speaks:

"As I said, after the 'Yes', in marriage there is no going back; except for one exception, and that exception always brings destruction to the relationship. I'm referring to betrayal, that's the only reason why some of the “ALLIANCE WARRIORS” can break up. And I don't need to exemplify the destruction of the relationship, because you all just witnessed it."

"Divorce is a serious thing, but it can be avoided," explains William Thompson, gesturing with his hand. "And as the old man said, “we cannot stop, because the enemy does not rest”. We have to move on, because the problems and the bills don't stop coming."

Liam, Anne, Noah, Sophia, William, Emma, Adam, and Elizabeth walk towards the exit of the rings' energy recovery area.

# COLLECTIVE TRAINING

It's already night at the “Swallow” base. Liam Cooper, Anne Smith, Noah Cooper, Sophia Johnson, William Thompson, Emma Thompson, Nicholas Henderson, Jennifer Henderson, Adam Scott, and Elizabeth White are gathered in the training area for recruits. Mr. Nicholas speaks:

"As I said before, life goes on. Tonight, the training of your recruits will be collective. I know that one of the fights was not held because of what happened before."

Sh. Nicholas looks in the direction of Noah, Sophia, Adam, and Elizabeth. he continues:

"But there will be no shortage of opportunities for this fight to happen. I make a point of being present when this feat is accomplished."

"Today's training is very important to see couples working as a team with other couples in random combat," explains Ms. Jennifer Henderson.

"Attention!" Mr. Nicholas Henderson orders, raising his hand and pointing to the training booths. "Recruits can now go to their places. Training booths are already scheduled for the same training area."

Liam, Anne, Noah, Sophia, Adam, and Elizabeth begin to walk towards the training cabins. William warns them:

"Today is just another training session, but tomorrow, it could be in real life. So, you all do your best now, so that tomorrow you have the best to offer."

"Remember, a couple never fights alone; for the challenge of one becomes of both," advises Emma

Thompson, clenching her fists.

Noah, Sophia, Adam, and Elizabeth give a thumbs up by agreeing with Emma.

"What my wife just said also applies to you, Liam, and you, Anne," William Thompson jokingly warns.

Liam nods and says:

"I already understand, I just think I need to fit in somewhere."

"I understand everything that has been said, but I'm not with the right person at the moment," Anne Smith explains happily. "But when everything is in its proper place, I believe things will get better."

Liam, Anne, Noah, Sophia, Adam, and Elizabeth enter the training booths in pairs. William comments to his wife:

"I'm worried about Liam, he's still shaken because of the last training at the “Eagle” base."

"I agree with you, my love, but things are not being easy for anyone, and there are choices that only the person himself can decide. Liam, like the other recruits, is still in the phase of planting the seed and, only later, reaping the fruit."

"This is the detail that makes all the difference, they have to be careful when making their choices. And Liam, like the others, is being very well guided, but it's up to them to walk their own paths, whether single or married."

"You're absolutely right, honey."

Liam, Anne, Noah, Sophia, Adam, and Elizabeth are already sitting in their seats in the training cabins.

"Sophia, we're going into this training like it's for real combat," Noah Cooper said a little tensely, putting his hand on his teammate's hand.

"You can count on me to take on any challenge," says Sophia Johnson, placing her other hand in her partner's hand. "Together, we can overcome any obstacle."

Noah and Sophia exchange glances and smiles. Adam and Elizabeth are also talking in their cabins.

"Elizabeth, I don't promise anything, but I'm going to do my best in this training," Adam Scott said, holding and kissing his teammate's hand.

"I know I can count on you, Adam," Elizabeth White said, holding her companion's hand. "This training is just another challenge to make us even stronger."

"Let's go together until the end, my love!"

Adam and Elizabeth also exchange glances and smiles. Liam and Anne are already in their seats in the training cabin, the two are having a serious conversation as usual.

"Liam, try to do your part, but working with me," said Anne Smith, trying to remain calm. "If you want to do things yourself, this is not a place for you."

"Don't worry about me, Anne, because I know where I belong. You, on the other hand, live in the fantasy of someone you met in a single training session," Liam Cooper said with annoyance. "Together we can do this; together we can do that; together we won there, together we won here," he mocks, gesturing with his hands. "What nonsense."

"Better than living in disappointment with someone you don't even know," screams Sophia Smith, losing her temper. "Get over it, Liam, and go live your life."

"You don't have to worry about my life," warns Liam Cooper in a lower tone of voice. "Because I know how to mind my own business."

"But if you've chosen to be here, you can't just think about your life, because this is a two-way street and not an individual one," explains Anne Smith, also in a lower tone of voice. "Think about it, Liam."

"I already told you, just do your part, and the rest is up to me. When I need your opinion on my way of life, I'll let you know, Anne."

"We're never going to win like this, Liam."

"Now stop talking and let's go to the training area, because it's about to start. Let's find the others."

Liam proceeds to the door of the training booth. Anne puts her hand on her face, shakes her head negatively, and wonders:

"Won't this situation I'm living in end? When will I go to this “Macaw” base to make the exchange, and then seek my true purpose? I know Liam isn't the person he shows himself to be, but if he doesn't make an effort to change that situation, no one else can do anything for him."

Anne emerges from the training cabin and meets up with Liam, Noah, Sophia, Adam, and Elizabeth in a forest. Liam pats Anne lightly on the back and jokes excitedly:

"With this delay, I thought you wouldn't come, Anne. And let's get right to it, the training is going to start, and I'm excited to show you that this time will be very different from the last few trainings. I'm going to show that I'm the best among everyone here."

Anne makes light of Liam and says:

"With these attitudes, Liam. You're not the best here or anywhere else."

"I just need to get to the Macaw base, find someone

aligned with my purpose, win the next training, and become one of the strongest 'ALLIANCE WARRIORS' that has ever existed," said Liam Cooper confidently and clenching his fists.

"You really want to become one of the 'ALLIANCE WARRIORS', Liam," said Sophia Johnson, impressed. "It sounds like you're really wanting to change."

"Brother, you surprise me with your attitudes," Noah Cooper said jokingly. "Why this ambition now, my brother?"

"I've already said, I'm giving myself a second chance, and I can show you that you don't need a lot of affinity with a training partner to become one of the 'ALLIANCE WARRIORS'. Even with Anne, I can achieve this feat if necessary."

"Don't include me in your troubles, Liam," Anne Smith said, gesturing with her hand negatively. "I can't wait to make the switch." Because unlike you, I want to make a commitment, I want to form a family, and yes, become one of the “ALLIANCE WARRIORS” and fight for the cause."

"Brother, be careful with these choices, because like I told you, you could end up hurting someone or even hurting yourself," Noah Cooper said, placing his hand on Liam's shoulder.

"My dear brother, Noah. Don't worry about me, because my heart has already learned what it can and can't do in a relationship," Liam Cooper said mockingly. "You know? So he doesn't get hurt," he removes Noah's hand from his shoulder.

Elizabeth calls everyone's attention, signals with her hand for everyone to be quiet, and says quietly:

"I didn't want to interrupt your conversation, but

there's something coming."

"It looks like training has already begun," Adam Scott warns in a low voice. "I'm not the leader here, but I want everyone to pay attention to what I'm going to say, because I've been through this kind of training before." he looks around, checking the place. "To win this fight, we will have to combine the skills of the couple."

"You don't have to say it twice, because I also know what that kind of training looks like," agrees Noah Cooper, also looking around. "And I just wanted to say that we still have a fight pending, Adam."

"Don't worry, Noah, because I was going to comment on it sooner or later."

"Men, always being competitive," comments Anne Smith, shaking her head negatively.

"And instead of you noticing the men, because you don't do your part in the fight, then I can do mine," Liam Cooper said, beginning to insult his training partner.

Anne threatens to punch Liam, but Sophia interrupts Anne's action and warns everyone:

"Attention! The things that had to come to us have already arrived here. There is something hidden in the forest around us."

"Everyone activate their energy protections and prepare for combat," orders Noah Cooper.

"Sophia and Anne! Let's activate our energetic protection in a triangular formation," orders Elizabeth White, looking at the two girls. "Thus, our protection becomes more resistant. It is a strategy that a society of couples uses to strengthen itself when they are surrounded by enemies."

"Understood!" Sophia Johnson and Anne Smith

agree at the same time.

Liam, Anne, Noah, Sophia, Adam, and Elizabeth activate their energetic protection. Women activate the protection of energy fixed to the ground and in a triangular formation. Anne, Sophia, and Elizabeth form a single, large ball of transparent energy that protects all three at the same time. Men activate their energetic protections near their bodies, their combat weapons, with the exception of Adam, they stand with their backs to each other and facing the bushes where their opponents are. Noah yells:

"They're coming!"

A group of android ninjas and android marines jump out of the bushes, the ninjas wield short-range weapons such as: swords, axes, spears and others. The Marines wielded long-range weapons such as rifles, 12-gauges, shotguns, and others.

"This time, I'm going to win in this training session, whatever the cost," says Liam Cooper, wielding his medieval sword and shield. "I'll show my worth in combat!" He enters a combat posture.

Liam with his sword begins to attack the Ninjas and the Marines and defend himself with his shield from the short and long range attacks of his rivals. Liam takes out some ninja and some Marines quickly.

"You rusty androids!" Noah Cooper said, in combat posture with his crossbow and his medieval barrier. "You shouldn't have challenged my mate and me," he winks at his mate.

"Together we are stronger, Noah," says Sophia Johnson, reciprocating her partner's gesture.

The androids attack Noah, and he dodges the ninja's

attacks, protects himself with his barrier from the androids' shots, and then shoots arrows with his crossbow, defeating several ninjas and marines.

"My mate and I are going to finish you all androids!" Adam Scott screams as he prepares to fight.

The androids also attack Adam, he dodges the attacks and then counterattacks the ninjas and the marines with boxing moves, capoeira and with some jiu-jitsu submissions, Adam also defeats many ninjas and marines in a short time.

"Adam, I've increased your stamina and your attack force," warns Elizabeth White, analyzing her options in the 3D image.

His bracelets begin to glow. Adam looks at Elizabeth, makes a heart gesture with his hands to her, and then smiles. Then some ninjas and marines with their short and long range weapons hit Adam, but they hit the energy protection, and nothing happens. Adam looks at the ninjas and the Marines, smiles, and starts another sequence of capoeira, boxing, and jiu-jitsu moves, and thus eliminates another group of ninjas and Marines.

"Noah, I've increased your speed and the firing speed of your arrows," warns Sophia Johnson, analyzing her resources. "The ninjas and marines are in greater numbers, but I analyzed the system, and it showed that their resistance is not very high. So I opted for a tactic of hitting a larger number of targets than concentrated and stronger attacks."

"Perfect, I wouldn't do it differently, my love!" Noah Cooper said, firing several arrows faster than usual and thus eliminating a larger number of ninjas and marines. "You are amazing, Sophia."

Sophia blows a kiss to Noah, and he pretends to take

the kiss with his hand and puts it on his chest. Then Noah looks at Adam and is impressed by the young man's abilities in fighting the androids. He comments:

"Adam, for a person who doesn't use combat weapons, you fight very well."

"I manage it the way I can," Adam Scott explains, finishing off a ninja android with a choke. "But if I'm still in a position to fight, it's because of the partner I have by my side," he says, looking at Elizabeth, and she smiles. "Without her, I don't know what I would do."

"I know very well what it's like to have a partner who is by our side all the time," Noah Cooper agrees, looking at Sophia as she analyzes her options in the 3D image.

Sophia, smiling, looks at Noah and gives a thumbs-up sign, and he reciprocates the gesture.

"I may not have a training partner, but I can show that I can overcome any challenge without having any kind of affinity with anyone," Liam Cooper comments to himself, even after listening to his brother and Adam's conversation. "I'm going to prove that there's no such thing as depending on each other," he clenches his fists as he smiles discreetly. "And when I become one of the 'ALLIANCE WARRIORS', I will follow my ultimate goal."

"Liam!" Anne Smith says to interrupt him. "Stop talking to yourself and try to connect with me so that we can fight together and finish this training once and for all."

"I can't wait to get rid of this girl, too," Liam Cooper said quietly. "In fact, she can ruin all my plans," he looks at Anne with a fixed gaze. "I can no longer continue by her side."

"Liam! Are you listening to me talk to you?"

"Yes, Anne, I hear you, because I'm not deaf," Liam Cooper said arrogantly and looking away from Anne. "You can't see that I'm doing what I can. Try to do something to help with this training as well, Anne."

"Liam is a difficult person to deal with," grumbles Anne Smith, taking a deep breath. "I can't do anything if you don't cooperate, Liam," she says softly and looks at Liam. "I used to be angry with him, but now, my anger is decreasing even when the two of us are arguing. What a strange thing, but let me see what I can do for this hard-headed Liam."

Anne begins to analyze her resources, and Liam begins to attack a group of ninjas and marines with his sword and defends himself with his shield. He looks at Anne and realizes that she is operating her resources, but nothing is happening. He complains:

"Anne, you're not going to say anything positive or do anything to contribute to this training. I can stay here all day, but I won't achieve Adam and my brother's achievements if you don't do your part as well. You and I just need to focus on the goal and move forward."

Anne continues to try to access her resources, but they have all been blocked, she warns:

"Liam, you're right to focus on the goal; But it doesn't work that way for the couple, as the two have to have a purpose together. You need to connect to me, so I can access my resources. I really want to do my part, but you need to stop this individualism of yours."

"Now, is it my fault?" Liam Cooper asks, finishing off another group of androids with his sword. "You just have to admit that you can't do your part, Anne."

"How hard-headed you are, Liam," complains Anne

Smith, getting furious and clenching her fists. "Let's work together to make this work, it's so hard for you to understand the purpose."

"I'm already doing my part," says Liam Cooper, fighting another group of androids. "Now I've come to win this training," he brags as he defeats a few more androids.

"I give up on you, Liam," said Anne Smith, discouraged.

Liam continues to fight the ninja and the Marines, but his sword and shield begin to fail. He looks at his bracelet and speaks:

"I can't believe it, the energy in my bracelet is already running out."

The number of opponents begins to increase, and some of them head towards Liam. Liam tries to defend himself and attack, but his combat weapons are disabled due to a lack of energy, and he begins to dodge the attacks of the ninjas and marines. Liam shouts:

"Anne, do something! You have to carry the energy from my bracelet."

"I'm trying, but you don't cooperate," warns Anne Smith, trying to access her resources.

Noah and Adam look in Liam's direction and see that he is in trouble.

"I need to help my brother," Noah Cooper said, looking at Adam and then at his brother.

"You can count on my help," says Adam Scott, giving a thumbs up.

Liam is cornered by the ninjas and marines. And when one of the ninja was going to hit him with an axe and a marine was going to shoot him with a rifle, Noah appears firing several arrows with his crossbow, he knocks down the ninja with the axe, the marine with the rifle, and the other androids around Liam. Adam, with boxing, capoeira, and jiu-jitsu moves, attacks other ninjas and marines who are heading towards Liam. As Noah and Adam defeat the ninja and the Marines, Sophia yells:

"Noah, here!"

Noah, Adam, and Liam look in the direction of Sophia's scream and see more ninjas and Marines attacking Sophia, Anne, and Elizabeth's energy protection with short and long range weapons. Adam comments:

"We opened a gap for our adversaries when we helped Liam."

"This was not a coincidence, but a strategy," explains Noah Cooper indignantly. "The ninjas and marines knew what they were doing, they pushed Liam away so we could help him and thus leave our comrades vulnerable," he clenches one of his fists as he firmly holds his combat weapon with his other hand. "This training system did what the androids would do in reality, they went straight to the weaker couple because the two are at odds."

"Let's attack these old cans with all our might!" Adam Scott commands furiously. "They shouldn't have messed with our training partners!"

"You don't have to say it twice," Noah Cooper confirms, wielding his crossbow and preparing for the attack. "I'm going to show these walking machines that no one messes with my Sophia. I'm going to finish you all off!"

Adam and Noah, with the features of few friends, begin to run towards the ninjas and marines.

# SOME TRAGIC ENDINGS CAN HAVE A HAPPY START

Still in the woods of the training area, Noah Cooper and Adam Scott continue running towards the ninjas and marines who are attacking the energy protection of Sophia Johnson, Anne Smith, and Elizabeth White.

"This is the end of the line for you!" Noah Cooper screams, firing several arrows towards the androids and defeating most of them.

"It's over for all of you, you old cans!" Adam Scott screams, attacking with his martial arts techniques and eliminating the remaining ninjas and Marines. "Never mess with my mate," he eliminates the last ninja android with a boxing move and the last two marine androids with a single capoeira move.

Then Noah, Sophia, Adam, and Elizabeth begin to celebrate the victory.

"We did it, Sophia!" Noah Cooper said happily and hugging his companion. "If it wasn't for you empowering me with these skills, I would never have fought the way I did."

"You fought valiantly for us to get to this result, Noah," Sophia Johnson said, putting both hands on her companion's face. "You're amazing."

"The two of us together are amazing," corrects Noah Cooper, hugging Sophia tighter.

"You're absolutely ruthless, Adam, my love!" Elizabeth White said, hugging her companion. "I don't know what I would do without you in my life."

"If I achieved anything in this training, it was because you were there, Elizabeth White," says Adam Scott, lifting his companion aloft, spinning with her, and placing her on the floor. "And I'm so grateful to have you by my side in the moments of victory and defeat of our journey," he says, looking into Elizabeth's eyes. "I know we are not perfect and we often even argue with each other, but if we put our relationship above any problem, barrier, or adversity as we always do, no obstacle will remain throughout our journey."

While the two couples celebrated the victory, Liam and Anne totally ignored each other, Anne sulking looks at Liam and walks away from him with strong steps and with her arms crossed.

"I can't wait to finish this chapter of my life," complains Anne Smith, gesturing with her arms.

Anne walks a little further and notices something wrong, she alerts everyone in the place:

"Guys, I think our training is not over yet."

Anne points to the left side, and everyone sees the trees falling and something coming towards them.

"And I can't even defend myself," complains Liam Cooper, looking at his bracelet and seeing it discharged. "I'm realizing that for me to achieve my goal will be harder than expected," he says in a low voice and gesturing his head negatively.

"Everyone get ready, because it's a great challenge that's coming here!" commands Noah Cooper, aiming with his medieval crossbow in the direction of the trees that keep falling.

Noah and Adam activate their protections again, position themselves with their backs to Sophia, Anne, and Elizabeth, and prepare to face what lies ahead. Sophia, Anne, and Elizabeth activate their protections, enter their features, and review the available options.

"Noah! This time, I increased the shooting force of his medieval crossbow's arrows and increased the stamina of his energy protection," says Sophia Johnson, selecting the options for her features. "Now you're going to shoot arrows that are more concentrated than fast," she explains, looking at her companion and making a thumbs-up sign with her hand. "This ability is more useful for tougher enemies."

"Very good! You're amazing, Sophia," Noah Cooper said, nodding to his partner.

Noah and Sophia's bracelet begins to glow.

"Adam! I increased his stamina and his ability to regenerate his energetic protection," says Elizabeth White, selecting the options for her resources. "I wanted to do more, but at the moment it's the best I can do."

"Perfect!" says Adam Scott, proud of his companion. "I wouldn't have done it differently, my love," he gestures a heart with his hands.

"I love you," Elizabeth White said quietly, and returned the gesture.

Liam looks at Anne, gestures with his hands, and asks:

"What about you, Anne? What did you do to contribute at this time?"

"I didn't do anything, Liam, you arrogant and brainless!" Anne Smith said impatiently. "And I realized that I can't do anything until you collaborate with me and with the goal of a partnership."

"I don't know why I asked," complains Liam Cooper, dejected and nodding. "It's no use, you don't do anything to help anyway."

"Focus on training!" Adam Scott commands with a tense countenance. "Who or what is to come has just arrived."

As soon as Adam finishes alerting the others, a rotting, deformed, and negatively contaminated rhinoceros emerges, felling more trees with its large horn.

"Liam, you need to connect with Anne now," Noah Cooper orders, looking at his brother. "We will need to unite to face this beast."

"From what I'm seeing, we're going to need everything we have and everyone here in this place," adds Sophia Johnson, worried.

"It's not my fault if Anne can't do her part in the training," Liam Cooper said, gesturing with his hands. "I already do my part of the training."

"Liam, now is not the time for us to argue," Anne Smith said, trying to access her resources. "I want to change our situation, but I need you to help yourself too."

"I don't need help," says Liam Cooper, looking at Anne with a straight face. "I know very well what I'm doing, Anne."

"Noah and Adam, you both have to be quick to eliminate this monster before the energy of my bracelet and Sophia's bracelet is also depleted," warns Elizabeth White, looking at the large rhinoceros. "And if that happens, it won't be good for us at all."

"What Elizabeth means is that the game is going to be over for us," adds Sophia Johnson, also looking at the monster and not liking what she's seeing. "And to think that this could be happening in reality."

"So, let's act more and talk less," Noah Cooper orders,

seeing the beast get even closer. "As Sophia mentioned, this fight may be happening in reality."

"Let's attack this monster with what we have!" Adam Scott screams, raising one of his arms with a clenched fist. "Honey, we're both going to fight “one”," he looks at his mate.

Elizabeth smiles and nods at Adam. he runs towards the beast and starts attacking it with punches and kicks. Adam, with his blows, even makes the great animal kneel with its front legs. The rhinoceros is furious and begins to counterattack Adam with its paws and horns. Adam dodges the beast's attacks by rolling on the ground and jumping on the animal, but when it jumps to attack, the rhinoceros hits him with its large horn and throws him over a fallen tree.

"My turn to strike!" Noah Cooper screams, running towards the monster and shooting arrows at it.

The great rhinoceros defends itself from the arrows with its head and horn and tries to attack Noah. Noah slides across the ground, passing close to the horn, and continues shooting arrows at the crossbow.

"This beast is very difficult. I need another strategy to fight it," said Noah Cooper, getting into a fighting position and pointing his gun at the rhino.

The rhinoceros begins to run towards the energetic protection of Sophia, Anne, and Elizabeth. Noah begins to run towards the beast to stop him.

"I'm not done with you yet, ugly thing!" Noah Cooper screams, shooting more arrows at his opponent.

"We still have a pending matter to resolve, freak!" Adam Scott screams, rising from behind the fallen tree and starting to run towards the rhino.

Just as Noah approaches to attack the beast, the beast hits him with its horn and throws it at Adam, putting the two out of combat. Then, the great rhinoceros reaches for the energetic protection and starts striking you with its horn. Sophia and Elizabeth warn Anne, seeing that her barrier is weakening with the attacks.

"Anne, you need to connect with Liam so that your bracelet regains energy," advises Sophia Johnson worriedly.

"If you keep going like this, your energetic protection won't last much longer, Anne," warns Elizabeth White, not liking what she's seeing.

"I know I won't make it if things go on like this, but I can't do anything else," said Anne Smith, discouraged and tired. "I tried to connect with Liam, but he doesn't open a loophole."

Anne's protection begins to fail under the beast's attacks. Noah and Adam, lying on the ground and very weakened, can only observe the situation. Noah looks at his brother and tries to scream, but only speaks in a weak tone of voice:

"Liam, if you don't connect with Anne at this time, it could be the end for her."

"We're just in a training session," said Liam Cooper, unfazed by the situation.

"Remember, Liam, this battle may be happening in reality," warns Adam Scott, pointing his finger at Liam. "Because it is in small gestures that we can already meet people of character."

"What I could do, I've already done," warns Liam Cooper, looking at the floor.

The great beast continues to attack the energetic

protection with its horn until Anne's protection fails, leaving her vulnerable, and Sophia and Elizabeth's energetic protection becomes individual again.

"For me, it's over," says Anne Smith, incredulous and discouraged. "I'm seeing my end."

"Don't give up, Anne," Sophia Johnson encourages with tears in her eyes.

"You can do it, Anne! Elizabeth White encourages with a strong voice. "You can do it!"

The beast, seeing that Anne was unprotected, stands on its two hind legs to strike her.

"On this road of life as a couple, you don't depend on just one member of the relationship to make it flow," said Anne Smith, seeing the large rhino standing on its two hind legs, approaching to attack. "But you need both partners for life to move forward."

Liam, Noah, Sophia, Adam, and Elizabeth watch the beast descend its great horn towards Anne. Then tears begin to flow from Anne's eyes, and she speaks:

"I don't cry because it's a training session; But I cry because, in reality, it could have been my real end."

The beast slams its large horn into Anne, pressing her against the ground. And so, when the rhinoceros raises its head; Liam, Noah, Sophia, Adam and Elizabeth look with incredulous looks at what they see. Tears begin to flow from Sophia and Elizabeth's eyes.

"You could have tried harder, my brother," Noah Cooper said sadly, unhappy and lowering his head.

Liam doesn't show any reaction at first, only tears run down his face, and he speaks in a low voice:

"I didn't know... I didn't know I was going to feel this

pain that I'm feeling now. This really could have happened in real life."

Anne closes her eyes and begins to disappear from the combat area. Liam also begins to disappear.

"My connection with Anne was so weak and bad that my bracelet didn't have a drop of energy to protect her," says Liam Cooper in shock. "Everything that happened was my fault," he clenches his fists. "My fault!"

Liam kneels down and starts punching the ground. Liam and Anne finish disappearing and return to their seats in the cabin. They don't say anything to each other, just remain silent, while the combat in the forest continues.

"This was the most real training I've ever experienced," Noah Cooper said, wiping tears from his eyes. "It feels like I felt in my skin what it's like to lose someone you love."

"I have to agree with you, Noah, I don't know if I could bear to be without Elizabeth," Adam Scott says, placing his hand on Noah's shoulder. "If someone has to die first, let it be me, because that's how it has to be."

"Noah!" shouts Sophia Johnson.

Noah looks in the direction of his companion and sees the rhinoceros with its large horn sharply attack Sophia's energy protection. Noah begins to run towards the beast with his crossbow wielded in his hand.

"I don't care if this is training or not, you're not going to get your paws on my Sophia!" Noah Cooper screams furiously and approaches the beast. "You damn freak, die!"

Noah and Sophia's bracelets begin to glow, and Noah's crossbow arrows change from pointed arrows to explosive arrows.

"Noah, you and Sophia together have activated a special mode of your combat weapon," explains Adam Scott, impressed. "This event occurs due to your willingness to defend Sophia and the size of her trust in you, that is, it is the husband's will to defend his wife and the trust that the wife has in her husband to be protected by him."

"Go back to where you should never have left, you fifth-rate freak!" Noah Cooper screams furiously.

Noah leaps into the air and fires the explosive arrows at the deformed rhinoceros. The arrows penetrate the animal's head, back, and four legs. Noah falls to his knees on the ground, and the arrows explode, sending pieces of the beast's deformed body everywhere and thus ending the training. Noah, Sophia, Adam, and Elizabeth begin to celebrate.

"You were amazing, Noah!" Sophia Johnson said, running and hugging her companion.

"I knew it was just training, but if I don't make an effort here, how can I protect her out there, in reality?" said Noah Cooper, looking into Sophia's eyes.

"You are and always will be my hero," says Sophia Johnson proudly. "Regardless of the circumstances, I will always love you."

Sophia and Noah hug each other tightly.

"You fought very well, Adam," Elizabeth White said, hugging her companion proudly. "I know I can count on you for any challenge in life, dear."

"Today was a day when my feelings were sadness," Adam Scott said in a trembling voice. "With everything that ended up happening, I felt the pain of losing someone special."

"Don't worry, my love, you'll still have to put up with me for a long time," Elizabeth White said jokingly and squeezing Adam's cheeks.

"And I make it a point to put up with every stage of your life, Elizabeth White, until the last breath of my days," says Adam Scott, touching his nose to his partner's nose. "I love you."

"I love you, too," says Elizabeth White, smiling.

Adam and Elizabeth hug tightly, and William comments, seeing everything that is happening on the screen:

"If a couple can't put up with each other's differences, how can they move on to a life in which two become 'one"? Liam and Anne are one of these examples."

"I have to agree with you, my love," said Emma Thompson, also watching everything on screen.

In the aftermath, Adam, Elizabeth, Noah, and Sophia are teleported back to the training booths. Liam and Anne are watching it all in silence. Until Anne can't contain herself, she looks at Liam and starts talking out loud:

"It's all wrong, you're a very difficult person to deal with, unbearable and proud, Liam. Today I found myself dying as if it were really because of you."

Liam, with a sad face, tries to speak, but chooses silence, and Anne continues:

"Liam, you don't have to say anything, but you need to listen a lot. You must be saying: "that only your training partner was missing," or you mean "now I don't need anyone because I can do everything myself". Is that what you meant? Are you missing that person who overcame all the challenges with you? But let me tell you. She's not here as you wanted. Accept it and put an end to this story."

Anne, showing that she is very angry, raises her fists and threatens to hit Liam, but she hits the back of his seat and is still angry, says:

"I know that you don't care about anything and continue in this training for a reason of your own, that is, an individualistic reason of yours. But I'm here because I believe in what I'm fighting for, I believe in a life where two people become one person; I believe in the life of a couple. I know your ex-partner acted in betrayal of you, even after everything the two of you have been through. And to make matters worse, you didn't even get a chance to find out who she was. But I have someone who is waiting for me, and I just need to get to him."

Anne wipes tears from her eyes, looks at Liam again, and continues:

"Liam, it's not because you gave up on something that everyone has to give up, too." I only ask you one thing at this point: help me get to my destination, and then you do whatever you want with your destination. I didn't want to admit it, but I need you now, and you know you need me to achieve our current goals, which is to make the partner switch."

Anne looks ahead, is silent, and crosses her arms. Liam is still disappointed and, with his head down, says in a low voice:

"Forgive me, Anne."

Anne has no reaction at first, looks at Liam, and asks calmly:

"What did you say, Liam? I didn't understand."

Liam looks into Anne's eyes and repeats:

"Forgive me, Anne. I know it was just a training. But when I saw you getting hit by that big beast. It felt so real that a pain came to me that I can't explain."

"A pain of loss, Liam," Anne Smith said, looking down. "I'm sorry too, Liam. I'm sorry for before, and I'm sorry I spoke to you like that now. I was just trying to relieve some of the stress."

Liam looks at the ground and confesses:

"There is no need to apologize, Anne. I deserved to hear your every word, I deserved to hear the truth. I blamed you for not doing anything to help, but the truth is that I couldn't work as I should. In my head, I knew I needed it, but since I couldn't, I tried to do it myself. After what happened today, I need to overcome my past and live my present to have a better future."

Anne looks at Liam and says:

"Liam, I need to confess something. Today, at the end of the training, I realized that this could have happened in a real combat. I realized that no matter how strong we want to be, sometimes we need help. Today I was scared like I never felt before."

Liam looks at Anne and says:

"I imagine how it must be, because the help that was supposed to come when you needed it, wasn't there for you."

Anne has a sad face and says:

"I think that's why I needed to vent to you, Liam."

Liam firms his voice, clenches his fists, and says:

"Anne, I know I've been a difficult person to deal with lately, and no one needs to tell me that. But from now on, I am willing to help you reach your destination, and then I will follow mine without looking back. I don't want any more conflicts between the two of us."

Anne smiles, takes Liam's hand, and says:

"I agree, Liam Cooper. From now on, you and I will work together until our separation in the exchange of partners."

Liam breaks into a smile, confirmed by waving Anne's hand lightly, and says:

"Anne Smith, I'll try my best to get to our destination." Let's fight together now and as “one”."

Everyone at the base was watching Liam and Anne and celebrated to see that the two had come to an agreement. Noah, Sophia, Adam, and Elizabeth celebrate as they watch Liam and Anne's scene from their training booths.

"How beautiful to see Liam and Anne understanding each other," comments Sophia Johnson emotionally.

"The two of them just needed an animal push," comments Adam Scott jokingly and laughing. "If you all understand what I mean?"

Elizabeth nudges her companion and looks at him with a straight face. Adam stops laughing and composes himself when he sees the way his companion looks at him.

"Now I believe my brother is willing to really change," said Noah Cooper, proud of Liam. "All is not lost in your life."

"In such a short time, I have only witnessed the two of them fighting with each other like I have never seen before among people who know the purpose of true couples," comments Elizabeth White happily. "I didn't think I would live to see this scene of reconciliation between the two."

In the recruit training area, William, Emma, Nicholas, and Jennifer also watched the whole scene of Liam and Anne.

"All is not lost in this failure to exchange couples from the 'Eagle' base", comments William Thompson, surprised. "This is something I didn't think I would see happen so soon.

"Sometimes we have to lose to give value," explains Mrs. Jennifer Henderson, impressed. "These two surprised me, but we have to be careful to recognize the value of the other before we lose them forever."

"But I always knew that these two were more than just picking on each other," says Nicholas Henderson, all proud. "I realized that from the moment I saw them."

"It took time for both of them to understand, but they finally realized that, in this life as a couple, they both need to give of themselves for the relationship to flow," explains Emma Thompson, smiling. "But as my mother used to say, 'Regardless of the circumstances, time will not stop to wait for me. The story of these two, as well as other recruits, is just beginning."

"You're right, Mrs. Thompson," agrees Mr. Nicholas Henderson, gesturing with his hands. "We still have a lot of work ahead of us," he says, clasping his hands and begins to disperse those nearby. "Everyone go back to your services and tasks!" We still have a lot to worry about."

The people who are witnessing the whole event begin to disperse. Anne and Liam look at each other inside the training booth.

"Is everything working in the training booth?" Anne Smith asks embarrassedly.

"I believe so," Liam Cooper replies, scratching his head.

"Liam, did everyone see and hear our conversation?"

"I also believe that everyone saw and heard our conversation."

"I'm very embarrassed," Anne Smith said, taking a deep breath and lowering her head. "I'm so tired, I think I'm at my limit."

"I believe in you, Anne," Liam Cooper said calmly. "But don't worry, because we spent this embarrassment together," he looks at Anne and smiles.

"It's a start," Anne Smith said jokingly.

Liam and Anne smile at each other.

"Training is suspended for tonight," Nicholas Henderson warns, raising his hand. "The recruits can go back to their quarters," he begins to hum happily, hugs his wife, and begins to dance with her.

# CONVERSATION UPDATE

Still in the evening, Liam, Noah, and Adam are in the male recruits' quarters. Adam is lying in bed, and Liam and Noah are talking and watching the movement of people and vehicles on the street through the window. The room they are in is on the fourth floor.

"Brother, you were totally selfish in training today," comments Noah Cooper in a serious tone of voice. "But at the end of it all, you changed the situation as a person of true character," he changes his tone of voice to one of playfulness.

Adam sits up on the bed, stretches out, and says in a louder voice:

"I'm very tired of all these trainings. These workouts are very real. I'm impressed. And I'll say one thing: if I managed to get here, it's because of the partner I have. Without Elizabeth, I think I would have given up at the beginning of these trainings."

"At this point, I have to agree with you, Adam," Noah Cooper admits, looking at Adam. "If I got where I am, it's because of Sophia, she's my reason to keep going every day."

Adam lies on the bed again, looks in the direction of Liam and Noah, and says:

"Liam, you really went through a shame today that no one wants to go through. But for the cause for which we fought, this process was more than valid."

"I'll take what you said as a compliment, Adam," Liam Cooper said, looking at Adam and laughing. "But my advice for today is to avoid going through what I went through to realize how wrong I was," he says, looking at the movement on the street again. "Actually, brother, I have my own goal, but at this moment, my goal is to get Anne to her goal."

"Are you sure that's what you want, my brother?"

"My brother, Noah," Liam Cooper said, putting his hand on Noah's shoulder. "Today, Anne opened my eyes, she is absolutely right. It's not because things went wrong for me that things have to go wrong for everyone. I have a choice: move on or live with the disappointment of the past forever. And I thank you, my brother, for always trying to guide me, even if I don't deserve your advice."

"Brothers are for these things," Noah Cooper said jokingly and placing his hand on Liam's shoulder. "But Liam, I know you." It wasn't just your conversation with Anne that made you change your mind; it may have awakened something in you, but there's still something more."

Liam looks into his brother's eyes and says:

"You're right, brother. Today, in training, I saw that beast eliminate Anne from training. I felt a tightness in my chest that I can't explain. But it seemed like she was leaving because of my pride, because of my selfishness, because of my lack of companionship. It was as if she was leaving my life forever."

"I don't understand that ending, my brother, what do you mean by that?" Noah Cooper asks, confused.

Liam is embarrassed, amazed, scratching his head, and trying to answer:

"I mean... I wanted to explain... It's just that it could happen in a real fight, and Anne could die forever because of me."

Adam walks up to Liam and Noah, interrupts Liam, and adds:

"Liam, you're absolutely right. Anne was eliminated in that training session for everything you said. But, think on the bright side, this was a scare for you to wake up to life."

"I have to agree with you, Adam," confirms Liam Cooper more calmly. "But it's a pain that I don't want to feel ever again in my life."

"On the other hand, your brother and Sophia together acquired a special combat weapon and eliminated that monster rhinoceros," said Adam Scott, celebrating with punches in the wind.

"I saw that part of the training, it was amazing," says Liam Cooper proudly. "Noah and Sophia were amazing."

"I'm not sure what happened, because I knew it was training," Noah Cooper said, looking down at his hands. "But when I saw that beast trying to attack Sophia," he clenched his fists. "I couldn't contain myself and just wanted to prevent something from happening to her."

"I imagine what it must be like, Noah," Adam Scott said, lightly slapping Noah on the back and explaining. "But this feat, as I mentioned earlier, only happened because of your determination to protect Sophia and the trust Sophia has in you."

"And surprisingly, one day I felt the same feeling as Noah," Liam Cooper said sadly. "But I can't believe my partner had the same feeling as Sophia, because she left."

Noah and Adam put their hands on Liam's shoulder.

In the girls' room for recruits, Anne, Sophia, and Elizabeth also talk, each of them lying on a bed.

"Today the training was incredible! Noah fought bravely as always," comments Sophia Johnson excited and cheerful. "Noah and I are a great duo, the two of us together can achieve great things and therefore we will help our parents, the grassroots and the cause in the war against androids."

"I can't explain how proud I am of Adam, he tries a little harder every day and every day he makes a difference in my life," said Elizabeth White with a passionate and very proud face. "And as much as Adam says I'm everything to him; In fact, he is the one who is everything to me."

"Anne, today was another day of disaster for you and Liam," Sophia Johnson jokingly comments. "But since everything has to end, you both had to go through this whole storm to recognize that you now need to work together."

"Anne, tell us more about your partner. I want to know more about his story and what led to all this," asks Elizabeth White curiously.

Sophia and Elizabeth sit on the beds. Anne gets up, starts pacing, and starts telling her story:

"Everything started to go wrong when the system of the “Eagle” base could not form the couples correctly. Other recruits and I switched partners, and I had the misfortune to find a selfish, despicable, and proud comrade."

Anne continues to walk, puts her hands on her face in disapproval, and continues:

"He let me die in training! Okay, it was just a training session, but it could have been in real life. But the truth is, as much as I tell myself that he's not my training partner, that the two of us don't match, that we both just argue with each other, that we both have different goals, that we were both a mistake in the system; My feelings for him only increase without me wanting to. And now, to make matters worse, he has decided to be the companion who is willing to do anything to make our relationship work. Would I ask him to go back to who he was? Would he do it for me? That way, I would still think I can change my feelings for him."

Anne sits up on the bed, lowers her head, and puts her hands in her hair in despair. Sophia and Elizabeth look at each other with an expression that they are not understanding at all. Anne raises her head and says:

"I can't feel anything for him other than the desire to stay away, because there's no point in being different from that. The two of us have only had several disagreements so far, and out of nowhere, everything starts to work out."

Anne lowers her head again. Elizabeth approaches Anne, puts her hand on her shoulder, and says:

"Anne, actually, I was asking about your training partner, whom you talk about so much. Which, in fact, I don't know who it is anymore."

Anne raises her head, looks with astonishment, and with shame answers the question:

"Yes, it stands to reason that you're asking about David. He would die for me. We both went through a lot together, including that training for “singles without suitors”, we faced many challenges together. Everything started to get out of hand in that workout, but David and I stayed strong and fought together until the end."

Sophia gets up from the bed, walks up to Anne, and kneels in front of her. Then Sophia puts her hands on Anne's knee and says:

"Anne, be careful not to get confused about what you want and what is right."

"I don't understand why you're saying that, Sophia. I already know what I want, and I already know who I have to fight until the end. And that's the right thing to do."

"Anne, I'm just saying that the first thing we learn as recruits is to analyze each other so that in the future we don't regret it or want to blame someone else for our wrong choice."

"But once I say that, I don't know why you're telling me those words, because I know what a wrong relationship can do. And that's why I tell you, Sophia, Liam, and I just need to get to the “Macaw” base and do the companion change. And so, end this story once and for all."

"If you're saying, Anne, it's not me, Sophia Johnson, who will contradict you."

"I've never been so sure of what I'm saying and doing," Anne Smith said with a doubtful expression. "Liam and I just need to work together to at least get to our current destination."

Elizabeth gets up from the bed and says:

"Since everything is resolved, let's take a look at the window and see how the flow of people on the street is."

Elizabeth walks to the window and opens it; she analyzes the movement of people and vehicles on the street. Then, Elizabeth looks in the direction of the front building and sees Liam, Noah, and Adam. She gestures with her arm and shouts:

"Adam, I'm here!"

Adam looks, sees Elizabeth, and greets her by gesturing with his hand. Adam shouts:

"I miss you already!"

"I miss you so much, too!" Elizabeth White screams very happily.

Sophia runs to the window, sees Noah, and shouts:

"Are you okay, Noah?"

"The only bad thing here is that I stay away from you!" Noah Cooper responds by screaming.

Sophia makes a heart sign with both hands to Noah, and he reciprocates with the same gesture.

"I can't wait to get together again," shouts Sophia Johnson, smiling.

"They say that at the beginning of the relationship, everything is wonderful; but after a while, husband and wife can't even look each other in the face, because it's the same thing as going to war," comments Liam Cooper jokingly.

"I have to disagree with you, brother, because there are arguments in the relationship, but the couple can't let conflict speak louder than love, and neither can they let love act without the presence of reason," Noah Cooper disagrees in a serious tone of voice. "Now, talking about war. When soldiers are sent to a confrontation away from their family, where they are sometimes away from home for months, the first thing many of them think about is how he wanted to be with his wife and children and they can't wait to get back to them, even if many of these soldiers don't know if he will be able to get out of the confrontation alive."

"That's why we shouldn't see a couple as a whole, but each couple individually, because the real couple fights for each other every day, every moment, no matter how hard it is," Adam Scott said, clenching his fists. "Because a life together has to have a lot of companionship and understanding from both."

Then Anne appears at the window and looks directly into Liam's eyes, he also fixes his eyes on hers.

"What do you have to say now, Liam?" Adam Scott

asks, not realizing that Liam is distracted by looking at Anne. "What do you think of these couples who think that marriage is a momentary and uncompromising feeling and of the couples who claim that marriage is a struggle for two, where both have to fight for the relationship to flow every day, even if one of them has to give in to the other many times?"

Noah nudges Adam and points it at Liam. Adam stops talking when he sees that Liam is concentrating on looking at Anne.

Elizabeth, from her room, comments when she notices Liam looking in the direction of his window:

"Girls, have you noticed that Liam is looking at something on this side of the building?" And with that look, it even seems that he has found something valuable on this side of the building."

Sophia nudges Elizabeth and points to Anne. Elizabeth is impressed when she sees Anne looking at Liam. She asks:

"What happened to those two? How did they change in this way?"

"As we've heard before, 'Sometimes you have to lose something to see how much you've lost," explains Sophia Johnson, admiring the situation. "But that doesn't mean it has to be that way, sometimes it's better to recognize it before the worst happens."

"Anne, are you okay?" Elizabeth White asks, running her hand in front of Anne's eyes.

"I know Liam wasn't being sincere before; he was just hiding behind a character to get away from his past," Anne Smith replies on impulse. "But now, I see a different Liam, a Liam with feelings, and I wonder how his training partner had the courage to leave him for someone else."

Sophia and Elizabeth look at each other without understanding anything once again.

In the male recruits' quarters, Adam nudges Liam and asks:

"Liam, are you sure you want to change partners?"

"There are things that do not depend only on one, but on both. And the important thing now is that she's well and happy," replies Liam Cooper, still distracted and looking at Anne. "I just don't want to lose her like I did in that training. And I don't even know why my feelings are different with her; it was not to be this way, for I had plans for myself, but now I don't even know if I want to follow my plans from before."

"It must be the second chance you're giving yourself, brother," comments Noah Cooper.

As soon as Noah finishes commenting, Liam composes himself and stops looking at Anne. Anne also gets a little weird and stops looking out the window. From their rooms, Noah, Adam, Sophia, and Elizabeth are confused without understanding anything.

"I had a purpose and I need to fulfill that purpose," comments Liam Cooper, still a little confused. "I actually need to put things on the scale now and see what's best for me, or at least I think it's for me."

Then William enters the male recruits' quarters, and Emma enters the female recruits' quarters.

William talks to Liam, Noah, and Adam:

"Attention! Emma and I are teaming up with the “ALLIANCE WARRIORS” from the “Swallow” base to go after the beasts."

Emma, following the same conversation as her husband, speaks to Sophia, Anne, and Elizabeth:

"The beasts have been located in the city of the 'Lost' and we have to go there as soon as possible before they claim new victims. Don't leave here, no matter what."

Emma and William leave the two bedrooms. Liam, Noah, Adam, Anne, Sophia, and Elizabeth rush to their bedroom windows. Noah points to the street and Sophia gives a thumbs up by agreeing with him.

"I thought the orders were not to leave the rooms," says Liam Cooper.

"I'm not going to leave Sophia alone at this point," says Noah Cooper.

"And there's no way we can do anything with the bracelets if something happens, because we're so far away from our companions," explains Adam Scott.

"Well remembered, Adam," agrees Liam Cooper, gesturing with his hands. "And I have made a commitment to Anne, and I must fulfill it," he says, running out of the room.

Noah and Adam look at each other.

"Let's go after my brother, Adam."

"Yes, Noah, you don't have to say that twice!"

Noah and Adam also ran out of the room.

Liam, Noah, and Adam arrive outside the male recruits' building and see Sophia, Anne, and Elizabeth across the street in front of the female recruits' buildings. In the place, there were also "ALLIANCE WARRIORS" couples circulating from one side to the other.

"All at their posts!" orders one of the husbands.

"Extra vigilance tonight!" orders one of the wives.

"Noah!" Sophia Johnson screams as she walks past half a crowd of couples.

"Sofia!" Noah Cooper screams, running at Sophia.

Noah reaches out to Sophia, and the two embrace. Adam also runs up to Elizabeth, and the two embrace.

"Adam, I know I shouldn't leave the room, but I feel safer by your side," Elizabeth White said, putting her hands on her partner's face.

"I also wouldn't be able to sit around doing nothing in the room knowing I could be doing something for you," Adam Scott said with a smile.

Liam and Anne approach and greet each other without having physical contact. Liam and Anne talk animatedly.

"Anne, my promise still stands," says Liam Cooper, smiling. "We will fight together until we get to the change of training partners, as I promised", he says with a little sadness.

"Yes, of course that's our goal," agrees Anne Smith, happy and sad afterwards.

"Is there a problem with the two of us working as a duo?" Liam Cooper asks, noticing that Anne has changed her countenance.

"No, of course not, Liam," Anne Smith replies excitedly and trying to disguise her sadness. "One helping the other until we reach our goal, after that, each one follows their own destiny."

Liam and Anne smile at each other, but the two can't maintain the posture of joy for long, and soon, both show sadness on their faces.

"To me, the way things are going is more than perfect," Liam Cooper says with little excitement.

"For me, it's also more than perfect," says Anne Smith, looking away from Liam. "And that way it will be better for both of us."

Sophia looks at Liam and Anne and asks when she notices that they have a haggard face:

"Are you two okay?" You both look a little sad.

"Of course we're fine," Liam Cooper replies, changing his haggard face and trying to act normal. "It's this movement of people that is bothering me a little.

"Yes, now that Liam and I are getting along, there's nothing to worry about, Sophia," Anne Smith replies, trying to disguise her sadness. "It's like Liam said, it's the movement of couples that's making me a little dizzy."

Liam and Anne look each other in the eye, and Adam interrupts the conversation and instructs:

"Let us go to the elders' quarters."

"That's a great idea!" Noah Cooper agrees. "Let's go!" he orders.

Liam, Anne, Noah, Sophia, Adam, and Elizabeth head towards the old couple's quarters.

# BACK TO THE CITY OF THE "LOST"

William, Emma, and a group of "ALLIANCE WARRIORS" arrive in the city of the "Lost" in a convoy. Some members begin to get out of the vehicles and analyze the place. Everyone activates their wedding rings. The husbands already have their weapons in hand, such as rifles, 12-gauge, and others. The wives are looking at their available features in the 3D images. Couples are not using the energetic protections at the moment.

"Attention, everyone! I want to remind you that my wife and I are the ones who command this operation; we are the couple who lead this convoy," warns the husband, who is the leader of the convoy. "So, I ask everyone to pay close attention to our guidelines," he nods to his wife.

"Attention, wives!" commands the wife leader of the convoy. "You all already organize your resources with priority skills, be ready to help your husbands in combat, and be ready to activate energetic protection, because without protection, husbands can only use simple combat weapons, and wives cannot get the necessary connection to use the support resources for their husbands, you can only use secondary resources, such as analytics, flashlights, maps, compasses or GPS and other derivatives."

"Attention, husbands!" orders the husband, who is the leader of the convoy. "All of you be alert to any movement, ready to activate your energetic protection, ready to protect your wives, and ready to fight any imminent threat," he raises his hand signaling for the group to split. "Couples! Divide into smaller groups and cover a larger area! Mr. William and Mrs. Emma, come with me!"

William and Emma give a thumbs up and approach the main couple.

"Sir, how many animals have been located?" William Thompson asks.

"From the cameras we left scattered around the city, they indicate that there are two lions and two lionesses, and all of them are negatively affected by the androids' bioweapon," replies the husband, who is the leader of the convoy.

"Ma'am, did they show any strange behavior?" Emma Thompson asks his wife who is the leader of the convoy. "Since they were being used by androids."

"From the analysis of the images, everything indicates that these beasts are not acting as they should."

"From what I have analyzed, I would say that these beasts have been trained or partially domesticated," adds her husband, who is the leader of the convoy.

"That would be impossible," William Thompson said doubtfully. "Wouldn't it be?"

"I hope so, my friend," said the wife who was the leader of the convoy, a little discredited.

"But we can't rule out any hypothesis, as both the android ninja and the android marines are evolving their combat strategies," Emma Thompson said.

The group of couples continues to scour the area, entering houses, buildings, hiding places they find in the city and even climb on the roofs of buildings, husbands walk around with their combat weapons in hand and wives walk with a light scanner of their resources to make a more detailed analysis of the place. Willian enters a bar with his spear in his hands and analyzes the place with his eyes; his wife, Emma, enters right behind him with her light scanner. She moves around the place and finds traces of the beasts on the floor behind the counter and speaks:

"The beasts passed through here, maybe they were after the inhabitants who were hiding.

"But this is very strange," William Thompson said suspiciously. "There's nothing in this town for the beasts to come back here," he rubs his head. "Let's join the others, Emma."

"Okay!"

Emma and William leave the bar and join the convoy leader couple again.

"Did you find anything, Mr. Thompson?" asks the husband, who is the leader of the convoy. "Any clue of these beasts?"

"According to the analyses done by my wife, only traces of the animals and nothing else."

"That doesn't make sense," comments the wife who is the leader of the convoy. "We surrounded the entire area before invading the place."

"Unless the beasts are gone before we get here," Emma Thompson deduces with a worried face.

Then, a couple runs to the couple who is the leader of the convoy, and the distressed husband says:

"Sir, we searched the entire city and found footprints of the beasts that come out of this area and lead to our 'Swallow' base.

"We fell into a trap so that our base would be vulnerable, because when they sent us to this place, the number of couples at the base decreased a lot," says the desperate wife.

"We have to get back as soon as possible," advises Emma Thompson worriedly.

The husband, who is the leader of the convoy, raises his hand and, commanding, shouts:

"Attention, couples! Everyone back to their vehicles and back to the “Swallow” base as soon as possible.

The group of couples “ALLIANCE WARRIORS” begins to run to their vehicles. Vehicles begin to leave the city of the “Lost” as soon as possible. Willian, already in the vehicle along with his wife and the couple who lead the convoy, asks:

“But what do they want with this whole situation?”

"Certainly, the androids must be looking to take advantage of the fragility of the base with the fallen couples and the reduced guard to attack," Emma Thompson deduces.

"They may be wanting to do the same thing they did with the main base, “Swallow”," deduces the wife, who is the leader of the convoy, clenching her fists.

"So let's go as fast as we can before these old cans can achieve their goals," said the convoy's leader's husband. "Speed up these vehicles," he orders loudly.

The convoy of the “ALLIANCE WARRIORS" follows as fast as possible through the desert.

# A BAD MEMORY

At the small base “Swallow”, Liam, Anne, Noah, Sophia, Adam and Elizabeth continue running towards the old couple's quarters, the six are crossing a square that had a fountain with a statue of a couple of swallows in the center.

"We're almost there," warns Adam Scott.

Anne stops running and points to an area where there is already a group of couples gathered. She comments:

"There's something going on there."

The town alarm begins to ring, and another group of couples passes by Liam, Anne, Noah, Sophia, Adam, and Elizabeth. One of the wives screams as she runs:

"We are being attacked by beasts that have been negatively affected by the androids' bioweapon!"

One of the husbands raises one of his arms and encourages his group:

"Let's put an end to these beasts!"

"That's weird, because the beasts don't attack bases or cities," says Sophia Johnson suspiciously. "These living beings even avoid this type of situation."

"These beasts are the ones that the androids have captured; they are not the same as the others," warns Adam Scott.

"These beasts chose a good time to attack, because the base is very vulnerable because of the number of couples present," comments Liam Cooper mockingly, and not liking the situation at all.

"What does that mean?" Elizabeth White asks.

"That this attack is not a random attack, but rather, a planned attack," replies Noah Cooper.

"Look, the main couple has already joined the other couples," says Liam Cooper, pointing to the place. "And this group of couples who just passed through us will also join the other couples."

"That's not good at all," comments Adam Scott with a worried face. "These beasts must be too dangerous for everyone to be gathered in that place."

And when the two groups of couples come together, two deformed and rotting lions and two lionesses emerge from the dark streets of the base, the couples prepare to face them.

"Surround the beasts, don't let these monsters spread around the base!" orders the leader husband gesturing with his hands. "Husbands, activate your combat weapons!"

The husbands begin to activate their combat weapons such as: swords, axes, spears, rifles, machine guns, 12 gauge, among others.

"Wives, you heard the command, form a circle around the beasts and activate your energetic protection!" commands the leading wife gesturing with her hands. "We can't let these beasts spread around the base!"

The husbands begin to use their combat weapons against the beasts and the wives activate their energetic protection in the form of a circle and forming a single, large circle around the felines, making the place look like a fighting arena.

"Wives, help your husbands with the resources available!" commands the leading wife.

Wives begin to empower their husbands with the available resources, such as strength, speed, and resistance regeneration, among others. Couples' wedding rings begin to shine. The husbands, with their combat weapons and the skills that their wives allowed them, begin to have the upper hand against the big cats, because when the animals are hit, pieces of their bodies fall to the ground and the four of them become dizzy from the attacks; But felines also had their strategies, as they have a great capacity for regeneration that prevented them from being finished by couples.

"These negatively affected living things are larger than normal," says Liam Cooper, looking at the physiologies of the four felines.

"And how do you know that, Liam?" Adam Scott asks, curious, and looks at the felines fighting with the couples. "You've seen some of these beasts up close."

"I've studied a lot about beasts that have been affected by the androids' bioweapon," Liam Cooper replies, bragging. "And these beasts are outside of the normal standard due to their size near the couples, because in the videos and books, these beasts are smaller compared to humans and larger when compared to living beings before they are affected by the android bioweapon."

"My brother is right, these monsters are different from other negatively affected living things," Noah Cooper agrees, realizing that while husbands have an advantage against felines, they can't annihilate them. "The regeneration capacity of these felines is greater than normal, because although the regeneration of animals affected by the biological weapon has increased, this regeneration is even greater in these beasts."

"Androids must also have something behind them," deduces Sophia Johnson.

The combat continues, and the felines begin to turn

the fight and have the advantage against the “ALLIANCE WARRIORS” couples. The husbands begin to lose energy from their wedding rings, and the beasts hit them with several blows of their paws, leaving them out of the fight. Then, the beasts attack the wives' energy protection to try and escape the enclosed area.

"Wives, resist!" orders the leader wife pointing to her wedding ring for protection and pushing with her hands to keep the energetic protection activated. "We can't let these beasts escape."

"In the situation we are in, it will take longer to recharge our resources to allow our husbands to regenerate," warns one of the wives, also pushing to keep the energetic protection activated. "Because we're using a lot of energy to keep the power protection active."

The four felines continue to attack the energy protection with their bodies and paws to escape the place.

"We need to do something to help the 'ALLIANCE WARRIORS," said Adam Scott worriedly.

"That's why I enlisted," Noah Cooper said, clenching his fists. "To become one of the 'ALLIANCE WARRIORS'. Let's help!" He raises one of his arms.

"Count on me!" Sophia Johnson screams with great hope. "I still believe in the strength of the couple."

"The good thing about all of this is that we're going to start the battle saving energy, because we won't have to go to the beasts," Liam Cooper comments mockingly. "Look there."

Liam points his finger in the direction of the beasts, and everyone sees the wives' energy protections begin to fail. One of the male lions jumps up and goes through the energy guard. Adam and Elizabeth begin to run towards the lion.

"Wives!" Adam Scott screams as he runs. "Keep trapping the other three felines. Let's try to take down this beast here."

The wives, not knowing what to do, look at each other.

"But they are still recruits," comments one of the worried wives. "This beast that escaped is too dangerous for them to face alone."

"They are just beginning this journey," says another wife, impressed by the attitude of the recruits. "But I have to admit that they have guts."

"We have to trust these recruits now, because if the three beasts escape as well, it will be total chaos," says the leading wife in a firm voice. "We need to buy time until our husbands are ready for combat again."

The leader husband, lying on the floor, looks at Liam, Anne, Noah, Sophia, Adam, and Elizabeth, gives a thumbs-up sign with his hand, and speaks:

"We count on you, recruits. Because in a fight, often the affinity between the couple counts more than the time they spend together, because many couples have their bodies next to each other, but the mind is elsewhere."

All the wives nod their heads, confirming what the main husband said.

"Recruits, you can do this, but don't forget, for couples to succeed in life, you both need to work as 'one'," encourages the leader's wife, looking at Adam, Elizabeth, Liam, Anne, Noah, and Sophia. "We count on all of you," the main wife looks at the wives and orders. "Wives! Focus on energy protection!"

Wives focus on energetic protection again. Noah, Sophia, Liam, and Anne join Adam and Elizabeth, and the six run towards the lion.

"What I found strangest this time is that neither Anne nor Liam was mad when they called them a couple," comments Adam Scott as he ran.

"Seriously, you're going to be thinking about that right now," Noah Cooper said, laughing. "We have a bigger problem to worry about right now," he says, looking at the lion.

Liam and Anne look at each other and smile as they run towards the beast. The big cat wastes no time and starts running towards the recruits.

"Now! Everyone activating the energy protection and preparing for combat," commands Noah Cooper activating his protection.

"Girls! We will give the necessary support to our partners and put an end to this aberration," says Sophia Johnson.

Elizabeth, Sophia, and Anne stop running and activate their energetic protection, then begin to access the available features of their bracelets.

"All of us together can overcome this beast!" Elizabeth White screams with excitement. "We will show why two become 'one'."

"Girls! Enable endurance and agility in your partners", commands Sophia Johnson, selecting the options of your resources. "Don't forget, as much as our partners have to sacrifice themselves for us, we have to motivate them with everything we have to offer, because if one falls, both fall."

"Leave it to me, I get the message!" says Elizabeth White, selecting the options of her resources. "We will make the most of the update of our bracelets."

The recruits' bracelets begin to glow. Adam runs in front of Liam and Noah and communicates with his companion through the bracelet:

"Elizabeth!" Add strength for me.

"Positive, Adam! But after that, I will be without resources until my bracelet recharges again."

"We'll have to take a chance anyway, as I'll try to immobilize the beast for Noah and Liam to attack it. It's all or nothing now!"

Adam and Elizabeth's bracelet begins to glow once again. Adam jumps on the lion, climbs on its back, and holds it by the mane. Adam has a hard time holding the beast, as his body and mane were crumbling and regenerating at the same time. The big cat starts jumping like a rodeo bull.

"I don't know if it was a good idea, because this thing is falling apart and regenerating at the same time really fast," Adam Scott said, still trying to stay on top of the beast as rotten pieces stick to his hands. "Yuck."

"Let's make your effort count, Adam!" Noah Cooper said, activating his crossbow and starting to shoot arrows at the big lion. "We're going to finish you off, you freak!"

Some arrows pierced the beast's body, and others plunged into its limbs of his body.

"Watch out for me, Noah!" Adam Scott screams with a look of astonishment after some arrows have passed close to his body. "Instead of you killing this beast, you'll end up killing me."

"It's all under control," says Noah Cooper, scratching

his head. "Or at least I think it's all under control," he says in a low voice.

"I still intend to marry Elizabeth," warns Adam Scott, still trying to hold on to the great lion. "Calm down, little horse, because if you keep jumping like that, you're going to end up knocking down the rodeo champion here."

Elizabeth gives a smile, makes a heart sign with her hands to Adam, and then screams:

"My biggest dream is to marry you, Adam Scott! I love you, but try to stay alive, please!"

The lion manages to grab Adam with its mouth, the beast shakes him from side to side, and then throws him into a stationary car. Adam collides with the vehicle, crushing it and spinning it with the wheels up.

"I'm at my limit," Adam said, standing up and showing that he is exhausted. "I have to admit, this lion is very strong."

"This beast has definitely been modified, because even in the hardest training, there are no challenges like this," Noah Cooper said, shooting arrows at the big cat as he ran around it.

The lion attacks Noah with its paw and throws him against the wall of a store. Noah breaks the wall and falls on top of the tables and chairs.

"Now it's my turn!" Liam Cooper said, activating his sword and shield and starting to run towards the big cat. "I'm counting on you, Anne! This time, we will fight as a true duo."

Liam goes on the attack with his sword and shield, but when he goes to attack the beast, his weapons begin to fail.

"What's going on?" Liam Cooper asks without understanding anything. "This time, I want to do it differently from the other times. I want to do what's right."

The large lion approaches Liam and attacks him with a paw, throwing him into the fountain with the statue of a pair of swallows. Liam, exhausted, leans over the edge of the fountain and looks in Anne's direction. Liam sees that Anne's energy protection is failing and he also sees a look of fear on her face.

"Anne still doesn't trust me," Liam comments quietly. "And I don't blame you, because I was very irresponsible and immature in the last few days by your side."

Anne remembers the rhino killing her in training. She sees the great horn of the beast coming towards her and cries out:

"I can't do it alone! He's going to kill me! I don't want to die!"

Sophia and Elizabeth look at Anne and try to encourage her.

"You need to focus on combat, Anne," encourages Sophia Johnson.

"You can do it, Anne!" encourages Elizabeth White.

"I died once, and I know what it's like," said Anne Smith, pale and frightened. "Or at least I came close to knowing what death is in that last training."

The lion looks at Anne, Sophia, and Elizabeth and starts running towards them.

"Noah!" Sophia Johnson screams.

The lion jumps with his arms outstretched, his claws bared and ready to grab the three recruits at once. But as he approaches, Noah appears with his back to Sophia, Elizabeth, and Anne and, facing the beast, Noah shouts:

"Don't mess with my Sophia, you damn freak!"

Sophia and Noah's bracelets begin to glow, and the crossbow's arrows are modified. Noah aims his crossbow with explosive arrows at the great lion and fires several shots at the lion, causing a large explosion at the site.

"Noah and Sophia have activated the special combat weapon again," Adam Scott comments enthusiastically. "These two are amazing together!"

"Noah was able to activate the special of his combat weapon because of his desire to protect Sophia and thanks to the trust Sophia has in him," comments Liam Cooper looking at Anne and seeing that she is still afraid. "And Anne doesn't feel the same security by my side because of the mistakes I've made," he looks sad.

Noah, Sophia, Anne, Liam, Adam, Elizabeth, the other lion, the two lionesses and the couples from "ALLIANCE WARRIORS" just watch the explosion. And as soon as the smoke clears, everyone sees a part of the lion lying on the ground and other pieces of it falling everywhere.

"Noah and Sophia did it!" Elizabeth White said happy and celebrating. "These two together represent true couples."

"Noah and Sophia are a real couple," Adam Scott says, celebratingly. "Like I said, they're amazing!"

"You two make a great duo, my brother," comments Liam Cooper discreetly.

Everyone starts to celebrate, except Anne, who is still in shock. Then the lion and the two lionesses become enraged and begin to attack the wives' energy protections with more fury.

"Attention, wives! Focus on your energetic protection," orders the leading wife. "We still have three beasts to eliminate.

"Our resources are still having difficulty recharging because of the attacks on our energy protection," warns one of the wives.

The leader's husband, lying on the floor, tries to get up, but, still weak, he can't and falls to the ground again and says:

"Wives, I know it hasn't been easy, but you have to resist with your energetic protection until I and the other husbands are ready for combat."

The wives nod their heads. The three felines continue to attack the energetic protection and, once again, the protection begins to fail. Wives begin to have difficulty maintaining energetic protection.

"Wives, we need to resist as long as we can," orders the leading wife, pushing with her hands to maintain protection.

The wives even kneel on the ground and with their rings try to keep the energetic protection activated, but when the three beasts attack at the same time, the wives' energetic protections break throwing the wives away from the place. The two lionesses begin to run towards their wives, who were a little stunned by the impact.

"Attention husbands! You know what to do in these situations!" commands the leader's husband by fiddling with his wedding ring.

All husbands use the last energy of their wedding rings and teleport their wives to the walls of the base. The wives are out of reach of the two lionesses and safe at the moment, but the husbands are even more exhausted and totally vulnerable, lying on the floor.

"Now we can die, because our wives still have one more chance to survive," said the leader's husband, smiling.

One of the husbands raises his head and says:

"I completely agree, sir. It has been good to serve alongside all of you and especially alongside my beloved wife."

The husband lays his head on the floor and starts laughing.

# THE PROMISE HAS TO BE FULFILLED

The combat at the small base "Swallow" continues. Husbands are still lying on the floor and vulnerable; Lionesses get lost at first when they see that their targets (wives) have disappeared out of nowhere. But then the two beasts focus on the vulnerable husbands and start running towards them. The wives observe the whole situation from the top of the walls.

"Wives, we must prevent these beasts from reaching our husbands," said the leading wife, clenching her fists. "I know! These decalcified females aren't going to get their paws on our husbands," she sees a pile of rocks, runs to the spot, and starts throwing them at the beasts.

The other wives do the same and thus catch the attention of the two lionesses. The two beasts get even angrier, give up going after their husbands, run to the walls, and start climbing them. The wives continue to throw stones at the animals and prevent them from climbing the walls. The main husband, with difficulty, starts laughing.

"I love my wife," the main husband proudly comments. "Only she can have this crazy idea of throwing stones at the beasts."

"I'm very grateful that your wife has this idea, sir," says one of the husbands, seeing the two lionesses trying to scale the great wall. "Because it means I can still get a second chance to see my wife, because I thought a few minutes ago would be the end of me."

All the husbands start laughing. The male lion sees the two lionesses climb the wall, but then he looks in the direction of the six recruits and the other dead lion. Liam and Adam are joined by Noah, Sophia, Elizabeth, and Anne. Noah, perceiving the danger, warns:

"Guys, I think we have problems."

The six look in the direction of the lion. The great beast lets out a great roar and starts running towards the recruits.

"Brother, don't you and Sophia have another special one stored in these bracelets?" Liam Cooper asks with a look of astonishment and seeing the angry lion coming towards him.

"Brother, this time, Sophia and I owe you a special one."

"Let's get ready for the showdown, because the beast is approaching," warns Sophia Johnson as she prepares to fight.

"Recruits, all activating the energy protection," orders Elizabeth White, fiddling with her bracelet.

The six recruits try to activate their bracelets, but the bracelets are depleted and they barely activate the energetic protections and it already falls apart.

"Everyone pay attention!" Adam Scott said it with an idea. "Let's split up and run as a couple until the bracelets recharge," he looks in the direction of the lion. "We can confuse this beast and buy time."

"Have you done this before, Adam?" Liam Cooper asks incredulously. "I ask you if you've ever done this in real combat or in any training?"

"Do you have a better idea?" Adam Scott asks, looking at Liam with a straight face.

"It doesn't hurt to try," agrees Liam Cooper, gesturing

with his hands for Adam to stay calm. "I just asked a simple question, you don't have to look at me with that psychopathic face."

"Then let's put the plan into action," Noah Cooper agrees, seeing the lion getting closer and closer. "Each couple goes one way."

Noah and Sophia start running to the right side; Adam and Elizabeth run to the left side; and Liam and Anne run in the opposite direction from where the lion was coming from. The lion stops running, looks to the three sides, and is undecided about what to do.

"At least my idea worked, I'm a genius in the art of war," Adam Scott said, bragging and running.

"That's why we should never lose control of the situation in difficult times," said Elizabeth White, smiling and running. "Because a focused mind always finds a solution to the problem."

"Honey, you said little, but you said what was necessary.

Adam and Elizabeth hold hands and continue running together. Noah and Sophia also continue running, he comments:

"Adam's idea will help us buy time to charge the energy of the bracelets."

"This strategy seemed weak at first, but it has proven to be very effective, and it is this strategy that will help us win," said Sophia Johnson enthusiastically. "Even in difficult times, we have to keep hope and believe that everything will be solved."

Noah and Sophia smile at each other and continue running. Liam and Anne also keep running, he says:

"Anne, don't stop running! The lion is still undecided where to start hunting."

"Positive, Liam, I'm not going to stop running."

Liam and Anne look at each other and continue running. The lion continues to look in all three directions without knowing where to go, but it doesn't take long, and it focuses on Noah. The big cat starts running towards Noah and Sophia.

"The lion wasn't undecided; he was just looking for me, because I was the one who killed his friend," Noah Cooper said, noticing the situation.

"Noah, don't forget that I also have my fault in this event."

"Sophia, if this beast gets to us, I want you to run as far as you can."

"Noah, I know very well what you would be able to do for me, but never ask me to abandon you. We are both "one"."

Noah starts smiling, nods, and says:

"You're right, Sophia. We are both "one" now and forever."

"Noah, in a few minutes our bracelets will be charged and we'll be back to fight that beast."

"Once again, you're right, Sophia."

Noah and Sofia keep running, and the lion keeps running in the same direction as them. Adam, Elizabeth, Liam, and Anne stop running and watch what's going on.

"I need to help my brother. This beast is very fast and will catch up with both of them in no time," said Liam Cooper, looking around and seeing a motorcycle adapted to ride in the desert lying on the ground. "It doesn't hurt to try."

Liam runs to the motorcycle, lifts it, and starts the motorcycle when he sees that the key is in the ignition. The lion begins to approach Noah and Sofia. Liam, on the motorcycle, begins to approach the beast. And when the lion jumps up to attack Noah and Sophia, Noah turns to defend Sophia, and she closes her eyes and hugs Noah from behind. But Liam arrives in time, jumps off the bike, and the bike hits the lion, knocking him down. Sophia opens her eyes and sees the lion lying down and moving from side to side, she also sees Liam lying on the ground and thanks:

"Liam, you helped us, I'm very grateful. This is the attitude of a true member of the "ALLIANCE WARRIORS."

Liam gets up from the floor and asks his brother and Sophia:

"How are you two?"

Noah runs over and hugs his brother.

"We're fine thanks to you, Liam," replies Sophia Johnson with great gratitude. "You're back to being the real Liam Cooper, and that's a good sign."

"What you did was pretty crazy, brother," Noah Cooper said, laughing and lightly slapping his brother on the back.

"Noah wanted to say 'thank you for helping us, brother," Sophia Johnson thanks once again in a joking tone.

"It feels like you're trying hard to change, brother," Noah Cooper notes, all proud of his brother. "I realized that you are willing to end what hurts you."

"I'm just doing my part and trying to move on, brother.

"Now, let's leave the conversation for another time,"

advises Sophia Johnson, looking at the lion and seeing that it is recovering. "Because our feline friend is about to get up."

Noah, Sophia, and Liam start running towards Anne. The four join, and then the lion gets up, looks in the direction of the four recruits, and furiously starts running towards them.

"It's time to use Adam's strategy again," says Liam Cooper, not liking to see the feline approaching. "And we have to use this strategy as soon as possible."

"It doesn't hurt to try one more time," said Sophia Johnson, worried.

Noah and Anne agree with Sophia and Liam. Noah and Sophia run to one side, and Liam and Anne run the other way and towards Adam and Elizabeth. Liam jokes about the situation:

"Let's confuse this stupid animal again."

But this time, the lion focuses directly on Liam. The beast begins to run towards Liam and Anne. Liam seems surprised to see the feline's decision and comments:

"I think he didn't like that bike very much, because he didn't even stop to think about what to do."

Liam and Anne continue running and the lion begins to get closer and closer. Anne stumbles and falls and Liam returns to help her.

"Anne, we can't run away from this beast anymore," said Liam Cooler, seeing that the lion is very close. "This damn feline is approaching very fast."

Anne pulls Liam by the arm and looks him in the eyes. Liam looks back and she says:

"Liam, I'm sorry, but I can't help you in combat. The

memories of the training keep coming to my mind. I can't concentrate."

Liam puts his hand on Anne's shoulder and interrupts her:

"Anne, don't blame yourself. I also wouldn't be able to trust a person after losing trust in them."

Liam smiles at Anne, looks at the lion, looks into Anne's eyes again, and says:

"If there's anyone here who has to apologize, it's me, because, once again, Anne, I won't be able to keep my promise to take her to the teammate exchange at the “Macaw” base."

Anne, with a face of astonishment and sadness, lowers her head and speaks:

"I understand you, Liam. Save your life while you can."

The lion begins to get even closer to Liam and Anne. Noah, Sophia, Adam, and Elizabeth observe everything from afar.

"They have to get out of there now," Noah Cooper said worriedly. "I need to help my brother and Anne."

"I wish I could do something too, but they're too far away," warns Sophia Johnson, looking around and finding nothing. "How could there be anything for us to use to get to Liam and Anne," his eyes fill with tears.

The wives on the large walls of the base and the husbands who begin to stand up slowly and still show themselves very weak, also observe the situation with the lion, Liam, and Anne.

"Now there's no time to do anything else," Adam Scott said, nodding.

"Even if we tried something, the beast would get to Liam and Anne first," says Elizabeth White with tears in her eyes.

Liam stands up, looks in the direction of the great lion, and then looks at Anne and says:

"Anne, pay attention. I'll try to buy you some time to get out of here, even if it costs me my life. You have to run as long as you can."

Anne looks at Liam with tears in her eyes, a confused face, and speaks:

"Liam, I thought you were..."

"No, Anne, I wouldn't do such cowardice to an enemy of mine, imagine for the person who made me open my eyes to life."

Anne wipes the tears from her face and says:

"Liam, but you're out of energy in your bracelet and out of your combat weapons. And if all that wasn't enough, I still can't do anything for you."

Liam smiles at Anne, looks in the direction of the beast again, and says:

"As I said, I will not be able to fulfill my promise to take him to the 'Macaw' base, but I will die trying to fulfill it. So, make it count, Anne."

Liam looks into Anne's eyes again and continues:

"Anne, I want to say that I'm sorry for everything I've put you through in the last few days. And in that last training session and with the conversation we had afterwards, I learned a lot. And I wouldn't be able to see you die again. I really wouldn't be able to live with it for the rest of my life. Don't ask me why, because it's a feeling that even I don't understand or could explain to you."

Liam clenches his fists and starts running towards the great lion. Noah, seeing this scene, cries out:

"Liam!"

Noah starts running towards Liam. Liam and the lion jump towards each other. Noah stops running and is surprised to see the scene. Anne, with tears streaming down her face, cries out:

"Liam!"

When everyone looks, they see the seemingly normal lion on one side, Liam on the other side holding his sword, and Anne with her energy protection activated. Everyone notices that Liam's sword has a larger, curved blade.

"Liam also activated the special of his combat weapon together with Anne," comments Adam Scott, impressed.

Then the blade of Liam's sword returns to its original form, Anne's force field falls apart, and the lion has its head severed. Liam falls to the ground, and Anne, crying, runs to him. Anne rests Liam's head on her lap and says:

"Liam, I'm here. Don't worry, let's get out of this together."

Liam, very weak, wipes away Anne's tears and, with difficulty, speaks:

"You were amazing. You managed to win. I never doubted you, Anne."

"We did it, Liam," corrected Anne Smith, still crying. "We both managed to win as 'one'."

"At least, I was able to keep my promise to buy time for you, Anne."

"And you'll keep your promise to take me to the “Macaw” base, Liam Cooper. I don't take no for an answer."

Liam and Anne hear Sophia scream:

"Be careful!" You two have to get out of this place now!"

When Liam and Anne look, they see the two lionesses coming towards them.

"Anne, you can still get out of here," Liam Cooper said, putting his hands in Anne's hands. "Run as fast as you can and remember, 'Make it count."

Anne carefully places Liam's head on the ground, stands up, and stands with her back to Liam and facing the two lionesses who were getting closer and closcr. Anne positions herself to fight with clenched fists, and in a firm voice, she says:

"I'll only leave this place if it's with you, Liam. And as I said, "You still have to fulfill a promise you made to me."

And when the two lionesses approach and jump to attack Anne, the two beasts are hit by a single shot from a ranged weapon and fall to the ground, lifeless. Everyone in the place hears the noise of the gun being fired.

"What happened?" Noah Cooper asks without understanding anything.

"It's the elderly couple, Mr. Henderson and Mrs. Henderson," replies Sophia Johnson, pointing to a building.

Everyone looks in the direction where the only long-range shot came from and sees Jennifer Henderson with her energy protection activated and Nicholas with his combat weapon in hand.

"It's not over yet!" shouts Nicholas Henderson, gesturing with his arm and pointing to the other side of the base. "We have more enemies in the base!"

When everyone looks in the direction Mr. Henderson is pointing, they see a group of negatively contaminated hyenas popping up all over the streets of the base, the beasts start running towards the recruits, the wives on the great walls, and the vulnerable husbands.

"It seems that tonight is not favorable for us," comments one of the husbands.

"We will have to react so that at least we die with dignity," orders the leader's husband, clenching his fists, hitting the ground, and encouraging his group. "Let's fight for our wives! Let's fight for our families!" He begins to make an effort to get up.

All the husbands present nod their heads in agreement with the main husband. Wives descend from the great walls and join their husbands.

"If we're going to die, we're going to die all together," says the leading wife, helping her husband up. "But we will fight as 'one'.

Couples activate their wedding rings with the little energy they carry and prepare for another combat. Noah, Sophia, Adam, and Elizabeth grow closer to Liam and Anne.

"Our bracelets have recharged some of their energy," warns Noah Cooper.

"Let's act like real couples of the 'ALLIANCE WARRIORS'," encourages Sophia Johnson vigorously. "Two fight as 'one'!"

"You can count on my help," said Liam Cooper, barely getting up from the ground.

Adam and Elizabeth activate their bracelets and speak at the same time:

"We're going to fight too!"

"I'm ready for the next round," confirms Anne Smith in a firm voice.

Liam and Anne look at each other and smile. And when the contaminated hyenas approach their targets to attack, the beasts are hit by long-range weapon fire from the convoy of the "ALLIANCE WARRIORS". The convoy arrives at the scene, attacking with all the weapons of its vehicles. Then, the couples get out of the vehicles and attack the beasts with their combat weapons. William and Emma run to the recruits and protect them from the monstrous hyenas that were nearby.

"Now you leave these beasts to us!" William Thompson said, throwing several spears at the approaching beasts and hitting others with short-range blows.

"Let's get rid of these hyenas!" Emma Thomson encourages with her energetic protection around her and the six recruits. "I'm going to increase the speed and damage power of your attacks, honey," she selects a few options from her resources.

William continues to fight the hyenas with his spear while Emma looks for more options from her resources. Some monsters that are facing William are hit by long-range shots. William looks over and sees Mr. Henderson helping with his combat weapon.

"Don't forget about both of us!" said Mrs. Jennifer Henderson, selecting options from her resources.

"My wife and I are also in the fight against these undesirable invaders," says Mr. Nicholas Henderson, firing more rounds with his gun to fight off the beasts, he also uses the bayonet of his gun in melee attacks. "You chose the wrong base to invade, damn monsters."

Couples who have just arrived in the convoy of vehicles also protect vulnerable couples from the beasts. The hyenas begin to be defeated little by little, leaving only the limbs of their bodies scattered everywhere. Everyone in the place begins to celebrate the victory. Anne and Liam embrace.

"We won!" Anne Smith said cheerfully.

"No obstacle remains erected in front of a united couple!" Liam Cooper said enthusiastically. "When a man and a woman join forces, they become unbeatable!"

Then, Liam and Anne, realizing that they are hugging, quickly part ways. Sophia and Elizabeth joke about the situation.

"Nobody saw anything," says Sophia Johnson, laughing softly. "Did you see anything, Elizabeth?"

"I don't even know what you're talking about, Sophia," Elizabeth White replies with a laugh.

Sophia and Elizabeth, still laughing, leave the place where Liam and Anne are.

"I could even complain that the reinforcement arrived late," comments Adam Scott more calmly. "But now that the danger has passed, forget what I was going to say."

"We can't complain, because if it wasn't for them, we wouldn't be celebrating this win right now," Noah Cooper said jokingly.

The leading couple who fought the felines approach the recruits.

"These six recruits have become true 'ALLIANCE WARRIORS'!" said the leading wife proudly. "Without them, we wouldn't be here now!"

"A round of applause for the new recruits who fought

bravely against the beasts!" said the leader's husband, smiling.

All the people started clapping and greeting the recruits on the spot. After a brief celebration, Nicholas raises his hand and orders:

"I know how good it is to celebrate a great victory, but I want special attention to the injured and extra security for tonight. Because we don't know when we might suffer another attack."

The couples begin to divide into groups, some go to help the injured and others go to the lookout posts.

# AN UNWANTED REUNION

The day has already dawned, and Liam Cooper, Anne Smith, Noah Cooper, Sophia Johnson, William Thompson, Emma Thompson, Nicholas Henderson, Jennifer Henderson, Adam Scott, and Elizabeth White are gathered at the main gate of the "Swallow" base.

"Once again, I thank all of you for your help against the beasts," Nicholas Henderson said, smiling. "My wife and I really wanted to be a part of the fight against the four felines, but we didn't have many options. Because we were trying to stop the hyenas from attacking on the other side of the base. Although it didn't work very well."

"But trust me, we both did our best to stop these beasts from entering the base," adds Jennifer Henderson, holding her husband's hand.

"I just have to say thank you, because if it wasn't for Mr. and Mrs. Henderson, I don't know if Anne and I would be here today," comments Liam Cooper, looking at Anne.

"I completely agree with you, Liam," Anne Smith said, looking at Liam.

Everyone in the room looks at the two of them, and Anne, embarrassed and with her hand on the back of her head, tries to explain herself:

"Don't look at me like that because I'm even embarrassed. Liam and I have just realized that if we don't work together, we are unlikely to achieve our goal."

"I couldn't explain it better than Anne has explained it now," says Liam Cooper, embarrassed and with his hands behind his back.

"If I didn't know the story of the two of you, I'd say

you're a perfect couple," William Thompson jokingly comments.

"But keep thinking about working together and the two of you will have a long road in life," advises Emma Thompson proudly. "And that your future partners think the same way you do."

Jennifer puts her hands on Adam and Elizabeth's shoulders and speaks:

"Mr. Thompson and Mrs. Thompson, I also wanted you to take good care of Adam and Elizabeth now that they have decided to leave to train at the "Macaw" base. The two still have a lot to learn in this life."

"I'm going to take care of them as if they were my children," Emma Thompson said, smiling.

Adam and Elizabeth look at each other and smile at each other, and Emma speaks with a straight face:

"I'm going to pass on the heaviest training sessions to both of them, they'll wish they had never left here."

Adam and Elizabeth stop smiling and look at Emma in amazement. She starts laughing and says:

"I was just playing with you two."

Emma stops laughing and looks at Adam and Elizabeth with a straight face again and says:

"But the training will be heavy for the sake of your recruits."

Everyone starts laughing, except for the six recruits who approach and look at each other.

"Jokes aside, but did anyone figure out why these beasts were different from the others?" William Thompson asks.

"I asked the lab staff to do some analysis of the

animals' bodies last night, and the results that came in in the morning are frightening," Jennifer Henderson replies with a straight face.

"What happened so badly?" Emma Thompson asks worriedly.

"In addition to the residues of the bioweapon that contaminated these beasts, the lab staff also found substances from the energy stolen from the alliances by the android ninjas," replies Mrs. Jennifer Henderson, still with a straight face. "This energy was altered and used on the negatively affected beasts."

"It seems that the ninja are trying to tame the negatively affected beasts along with the 'Lost' for a greater purpose than just using them as pets," said Nicholas Henderson, worried. "They are preparing for something much bigger than that to try to annihilate us."

"All of this that's going on is really bad, it wasn't enough for the android marines to negotiate with the “Lost” about wedding rings, now we have the android ninjas also joining the “Lost” to practice some kind of biological experiment on negatively contaminated living beings," said Emma Thompson, unhappy with the situation.

"According to the lab team, ninjas still don't have full control over the beasts; they can only lure the beasts for their macabre goals," explains Ms. Jennifer Henderson.

"Despite the failure to control these beasts, I believe that if the ninja continue to steal the energy from wedding rings, it won't be long before they reach their true ideals," warns Mr. Nicholas Henderson.

"We have to end this war against both types of androids as soon as possible, before they gain more combat power," warns Emma Thompson, clenching her fists. "And we have yet to figure out what the purpose of our wedding rings is for the android Marines."

"I believe we will find a way to end this war," William Thompson said, consoling his wife. "Because we have to keep hope until the end and keep fighting for our goal, the goal of true couples," he gives Emma his hand and the two look each other in the eyes and smile.

Then a fleet of buses arrives in front of the main gate.

"Why these buses?" Elizabeth White asks curiously.

"These vehicles will take the residents of the city of the "Lost" back home, because now that the beasts have been eliminated, many of them have decided to go back to where they left, that is, they still prefer the outside world," replies Nicholas Henderson with a bit of sadness.

"A lot of them don't mean it's all of them, what that means," William Thompson said cheerfully.

"That's exactly what you're thinking about, Mr. Thompson," Mrs. Jennifer Henderson says, gesturing with one hand. "All is not lost, as we have been able to recruit single people and couples from the 'Lost' group who do not know the true purpose of a couple. Now they have received guidance on the matter, as many of them were born in the city of the "Lost" after a couple of "ALLIANCE WARRIORS" abandoned the cause to live in a dishonorable world."

"Now they will go through a process of learning and training, and tomorrow they will be great warriors who fought for the cause," explains Mr. Nicholas Henderson, perking up and clenching his fists. "They will become 'ALLIANCE WARRIORS'."

"This is amazing! It's a sign that there are still people who believe that when a man and a woman come together, the two become one flesh, one person," said Emma Thompson very happily. "And this, it is not I who say, but the one who made the Earth, the Sky, and the Sea."

"My love, you said little, but you said what was necessary," says William Thompson proudly and placing his hand on his wife's shoulder.

Then, several residents of the city of the "Lost" begin to leave the base and walk towards the main gate to get on the buses, they are being escorted by the "ALLIANCE WARRIORS". A woman who lives in the city of the "Lost" complains:

"This is not life for me. This business of living for someone else is not my vocation. I prefer to live for myself without depending on anyone and live in a free place without rules."

The woman who is complaining tries to get on the bus, but trips and falls to the ground. One of the men from the group "ALLIANCE WARRIORS" helps her get up and get on the bus. William comments when he sees the residents of the city of the "Lost" complaining and other people leaving the "Macaw" base:

"There are really people who don't know how to take advantage of the chance they have, let alone be grateful for their lives."

"Don't be surprised by these attitudes, my friend," Nicholas Henderson said, placing his hand on William's shoulder. Since the existence of the world, ungrateful people have always existed. Now I wanted you and your wife to accompany me and my wife so that you could receive a gift from our “Swallow” base as gratitude for all that you have done for us."

William and Emma give a thumbs up and follow the elderly couple. Emma looks at the recruits before continuing walking and says:

"You six wait here and don't get into any trouble with the residents of the city of the “Lost”, because there are things that many of them don't understand.

Liam, Anne, Noah, Sophia, Adam, and Elizabeth give Emma a thumbs up.

"Don't worry, Ms. Thompson, we'll keep everything under control," says Noah Cooper.

"I even get scared when I hear someone say these things," jokes William Thompson.

Emma and William continue to accompany the elderly couple and Noah, Sophia, Adam, Anne, and Elizabeth begin to talk to each other, while Liam walks away from the other recruits when he sees a young man from the city of the “Lost” waving his hand at him.

"Liam, is it really you, my friend?" asks the young man from the city of the “Lost,” greeting Liam with a handshake and a hug.

"What are you doing here?" Liam Cooper asks quietly and looking to the sides to see if there was no one around.

"I left my city of origin and ended up in this city of the 'Lost' to solve problems about some sales", replies the young man from the city of the “Lost,” laughing and gesturing with his hands. "You know how commerce works, Liam," he says, slapping Liam lightly on the shoulder.

"It was even good for me to meet him here again,

because I need to clarify a few things on this subject," Liam Cooper said in a low voice and still looking around to see if there was no one around. "We need to have a serious conversation," he says, looking at the young man.

"I know, have you found the ideal training partner for our plan?" - asks the young man from the city of the “Lost,” showing that he is proud of Liam. "I knew you were going to make it, my friend."

Liam nods his head negatively and gestures with his hands, becoming a little awkward with the situation and demonstrating that it was nothing the young man was thinking.

"That's not what happened," Liam Cooper replies, a little upset. "And you can speak quieter."

"Calm down, my friend, I already understand the situation, you are still trying to find the right person for our plan," deduces the young man from the city of the “Lost,” gesturing with his hands for Liam to keep calm. "So, Liam, as soon as you can find a mate for our plan and you two become one of the “ALLIANCE WARRIORS”, you will come to me, because I have an ideal buyer for your wedding rings, your engagement rings, and even your bracelets. In fact, this buyer buys everything that comes from the “ALLIANCE WARRIORS”."

"Is this buyer an android?" Liam Cooper asks, indignant and holding the young man by the collar of his shirt. "It can only be one of those old cans, right?"

"I only sell the clandestine products and I don't ask questions to the buyer, Liam," replies the young man from the city of the “Lost,” taking Liam's hand from his shirt. "And I don't know why you're complaining, because you can get a lot of money in this business to live in the city of the 'Lost' as you yourself planned," he straightens the collar of his shirt. "You, me, and your partner who adhere to our plan, will live a life without rules and without commitment and still full of money."

Liam and the young man from the city of the “Lost” hear Noah's voice:

"So, that was your plan, my brother?" And still want to involve an innocent person in your dirty game?

Liam looks back and sees Noah, Sophia, Elizabeth, Adam, and Anne.

"Liam, I'm leaving now, because I don't want trouble with the “ALLIANCE WARRIORS”," said the young man from the city of the “Lost” running and getting on one of the buses.

"Actually, this guy only appeared at this time to complicate my life, which was going well until now," Liam comments in a low voice and watching the young man from the city of the “Lost” hide in the last seat of the bus.

"But what could we expect from Liam Cooper?" said Noah Cooper indignantly. "Because Liam Cooper is just being Liam Cooper as always," he walks around his brother. "And to think that I believed that you had really changed, my brother," Noah clenches his fists in revolt. "And you came up with these conversations about starting over and giving it a second chance. What nonsense, how foolish I was to think that you really wanted to change. In fact, your plans are already more than defined, aren't they, brother?"

"I believe that if I try to say something, you won't believe me," Liam Cooper deduces, lowering his head.

"You're right this time, Liam," confirms Adam Scott,

disappointed.

"Liam, do you have any idea how many 'ALLIANCE WARRIORS' or recruits you could put at risk for this ideal of yours? Sophia Johnson asks indignantly. "Have you ever stopped to think about it?"

"How many people will die for you to achieve your goal, Liam?" Adam Scott asks, still disappointed. "Will all of this really be worth it in the end?"

"Liam, the path to our goals isn't always clean, but that doesn't mean we have to be as dirty as our paths," Elizabeth White said, shaking her head negatively.

"Brother, when are you going to grow up and move on with your life?" Noah Cooper asks, still dissatisfied. "How long will you think about this betrayal you suffered without taking any action for your good?" He gestures with his arms. "And worse than all that, how long are you going to keep putting the weight of your problems on people who aren't guilty?"

Liam has a straight face and raises his voice:

"Now everyone is going to judge me?"

"Yes," Adam Scott replies, getting straight to the point, but then being in doubt. "Everyone is going to continue to judge Liam, right?" He approaches Noah.

Noah pushes Adam with his hand and then raises his voice:

"No, we're not going to judge you, Liam. In fact, you would have to be expelled from the corporation, because you go against the true purpose for which couples fight. You would have to be arrested for your actions."

"Look who is judging: "The exemplary brother who has never made a mistake in his life." you are not only judging me, but you are also already giving me the sentence for my actions. But they don't need to expel me, or judge me, or condemn me, because I was already going to leave this because that has no future for me. And yes, sometimes I'd rather live with the “Lost” than live with my own group, because the people in my own group have already betrayed me. And just to warn you, I can't be arrested for a crime I haven't committed yet."

"But this kid from the town of 'Lost' just cheated on you, Liam," comments Adam Scott, scratching his head.

Liam approaches Adam and explains in a low voice:

"What this young man did does not count as an act of betrayal; he just fled in fear of being arrested."

"To me, it still felt like a betrayal."

"Just forget about it."

"Liam, how can you live or sleep in peace, endangering the lives of innocent people?" Noah Cooper asks, still dissatisfied.

Liam takes a deep breath and, with a thoughtful expression, replies:

"In fact, I would not kill anyone or put anyone's life at risk like the androids or the 'Lost' do, or as you are all saying, Because I would only sell the things I have achieved, that is, I would only sell what is mine. There is a buyer for anything that is from the “ALLIANCE WARRIORS”. As you know, the equipment, vehicles, and weapons of the fighters are made with a superior quality material compared to the things that the world offers.

"So, you and the alleged companion who entered the scheme would leave to live like the 'Lost' and thus have a quiet life?" Sophia Johnson asks mockingly.

"Yes," Liam Cooper says naturally. "We would only live for the sake of living in this world."

Adam shakes his head in disagreement with Liam and says:

"This is dishonorable, Liam. Everyone knows that there is no peaceful life in the world of the “Lost”. They are not called “Lost” because they abandoned the cause, but they are called “Lost” because they live in dishonor with their neighbor, they live in prostitution, false couples betray each other all the time and glorify themselves for it. For these and other attitudes, they are called “Lost”. And you, Liam, would be just another person financing the world of crime.

"If it were a few days ago, I would say I don't care about the cause at all..."

Liam tries to explain himself, but is punched in Noah's face. Then Liam returns the punch, the two grab each other, fall to the ground, and start fighting. Noah manages to get on top of Liam, and just as he was about to punch his brother again, Adam pulls him over, grabs him from behind, and says:

"Noah! That's not how we're going to solve things! Even if the desire to take justice into one's own hands is great."

"You're right, Adam," Noah Cooper agrees, straightening his stance. "There are things that are not worth getting your hands on."

Liam stands up, dusts off his body, straightens his posture, spits blood on the floor, and shouts:

"Noah, FYI, you're right! I did some stupid things! Who has never done something wrong in this life? But in our trajectory so far, a lot has changed, including my goal and my way of thinking."

"Liam, you don't have to prove anything to me or anyone else; you have to do it just for yourself," Noah Cooper said with a straight face. "I'm tired of giving you advice, and you keep following the same path as always. I realize that there are people who have to learn the hard way."

Then, William and Emma arrive in the van from the “Eagle” base, the vehicle is all repaired and painted; and the elderly couple arrives in a V8 car with the symbol of a couple of swallows on the doors and hoods.

"All aboard, we will now continue our journey in comfort," William Thompson said jokingly.

"We now have quality fuel and parts in our vehicles," explains Emma Thompson enthusiastically. "We can drive without fear of stopping on the road."

Sophia, seeing the van in impeccable condition, says excitedly:

"What a wonderful gift you received, or rather, we all received."

The recruits begin to walk towards the vehicles. Adam speaks in a low voice:

"Guys, let's leave what happened here, between us. I don't think we have to take this matter further."

"I don't even know what you're talking about, Adam," Noah Cooper said, showing that he understood the message.

"I think this is better for everyone," agrees Elizabeth White.

The elderly couple approaches Adam and Elizabeth. Mr. Nicholas Henderson hands the car keys to the “Swallow” base to Adam and directs:

“Adam, Elizabeth, always seek to improve your relationship as a couple, because every detail can make a difference.”

"We're going to cheer you both on," says Mrs. Jennifer Henderson proudly. "Never forget, a couple can only win when they fight together as 'one'."

"When we vote here, we will be married and as members of the 'ALLIANCE WARRIORS, '" says Elizabeth White with tears in her eyes.

"I sign below what Elizabeth said," agrees Adam Scott, hugging his companion.

Noah and Sophia get into the van and sit in the middle seats. Liam, seeing his brother in the van, asks Adam:

"Can I come along with you, Adam?"

"Of course, Liam. As you said, “Who has never made a mistake?” We just can't forget that everything we sow, one day we will have to reap."

"What Adam means is that even if a person decides to change, it doesn't mean that they are free from answering for their acts already committed," explains Elizabeth White.

Anne approaches Liam and says:

"I'll go with you, too."

"Yes, that will be wonderful because we will have more company to talk to," said Elizabeth White with joy.

Liam looks at Anne and asks:

"Anne, you were the only one who didn't judge me for my mistake. Why?"

"Liam, I think we all make mistakes. In fact, we make mistakes on a daily basis, so we need a second chance to correct these mistakes and try to be better than yesterday," explains Anne Smith, putting her hand on Liam's shoulder.

"You haven't proven to me that you've changed with words, but with attitudes, so let's let time show who we really are." Anne walks towards the car.

Liam is surprised by what Anne said and comments in a low voice:

"I changed because of you, Anne. You opened my eyes. But now, I'm going to take her to be in someone else's arms."

Anne looks back, smiles, and jokes with Liam:

"Liam, let's go before they leave us behind. Don't even think about running away from your promise."

Liam smiles and walks to the car. Adam sits in the driver's seat, Elizabeth sits next to him, and Anne and Liam sit in the back seat of the car. William observes the situation and comments in a low voice to his wife, Emma:

"Didn't you notice something wrong with the recruits? Especially with Liam and Noah?"

"Honey, it is not good to constantly do what I am going to say; But this time, let's turn a blind eye to the situation and move on. I think at this point we all have a little bit of excess feelings in our bodies."

"I get the message, you don't have to say it twice," William says giving his wife a kiss on the cheek. "Let's go to our destination," he sees that everyone is ready to continue traveling. "Now that we are ready, we can put these machines to work."

The two vehicles leave the place honking their horns, and the elderly couple gestures with their arms and says goodbye to them. The lookout garrison fires shots into the air.

# THE REUNION

William Thompson, Emma Thompson, Noah Cooper, and Sophia Johnson in the vehicle of the base “Eagle”; and Adam Scott, Elizabeth White, Anne Smith, and Liam Cooper in the vehicle from the base “Swallow”, follow the deserted road to reach the base “Macaw”. The van was in front and the car was in the back. Days and nights pass, and they continue on the road in the desert. The group makes stops to sleep and have breakfast, lunch, and dinner. Of course, Liam and Noah didn't talk to each other, because when they passed near each other, they didn't even look at each other. The men took turns driving the vehicles, while the women took turns driving the 3D map. Sometimes, while one couple is active, the other is resting, and Liam and Anne even sleep leaning on each other. At night, the group observes the “Macaw” base from afar. Emma talks to Noah and Sophia in the van, and through the vehicle's communicators, she communicates with Adam, Elizabeth, Liam, and Anne in the car:

"Attention! We are approaching the “Macaw” base. Everyone should prepare for the inspection of the guards on duty."

The two vehicles approach the main gate of the “Macaw” base. In the corners of the great walls there were statues of macaw couples with their wings outstretched. From the Great Wall, one of the wives who is guarding the base, begins to analyze the two vehicles.

"That way, we all arrive at our destination," comments Liam Cooper, looking at the “Macaw” base.

"It took a while, but we managed to reach our

destination - says Anne Smith with joy. "After a lot of persistence, defeats, and victories, here we are."

Liam and Anne look at each other.

"After a few crashes, we learned from our mistakes," said Liam Cooper, still looking into Anne's eyes.

"We got up stronger and more experienced," adds Anne Smith, also looking Liam in the eye.

Adam and Elizabeth, inside the car, look back, and Adam interrupts the conversation and comments:

"If I didn't know the story of the two of you, I would say that you are a couple ready to go to war."

"Yes, I agree with Adam, I would say you're up for any challenge," Elizabeth White agrees in surprise. "But as I know the story of the two of you, I know that the end of this partnership is near."

Liam and Anne fall silent and look in opposite directions from the car windows. The wife, who is analyzing, gives a thumbs-up sign, and the husband gives the command through the communicator of his wedding ring:

"Open the main gate! Who we were waiting for has just arrived!"

Then the main gate starts opening automatically.

"We can move forward," says William Thompson. "The inspection has been completed."

The two vehicles pass through the main gate.

William Thompson, Emma Thompson, Noah Cooper, Sophia Johnson, Adam Scott, Elizabeth White, Anne Smith, and Liam Cooper are greeted with great joy by the “ALLIANCE WARRIORS” from the “Macaw” base, the “Eagle” base, the “Swallow” base, recruits from the above three bases, and other residents.

"These are the recruits who defeated the beasts at the Andorinha base," says a young recruit from the Arara base, curious.

"How amazing, Adam and Elizabeth are from the same base as me," says a young woman enthusiastically. "They are a perfect pair, because one completes the other's mistake."

"Four of them are from the same base of origin as mine," says a young recruit from the "Eagle" base. "Noah and Sophia are the champion recruit couple of our "Eagle" base."

"Now it's explained why these beasts didn't have a chance," said a boy from the "Macaw" base. "The best recruits from the 'Eagle' base and the best recruits from the 'Swallow' base were in battle," he starts laughing. "But now, these recruit couples will have to face the best recruits from the "Macaw" base in the next training. So, let's find out who is the champion couple of the moment and which is the base that has the best recruit couple."

One of the husbands of the "ALLIANCE WARRIORS" group from the "Macaw" base pokes his wife, points to Liam and Anne, and comments:

"Look there, honey." These two recruits must be the mistake of the beginning that worked in the end.

"Sometimes hope is born from where we have no hope," the wife said, smiling at Liam and Anne. "That is why we must never give up fighting for our ideals and for the cause of true couples."

Adam looks at Liam and Anne and comments:

"I think they're talking about the two of you."

"Liam and I worked together to achieve our goal of

getting here," explains Anne, embarrassed.

"There was nothing more than what Anne mentioned," Liam Cooper explains, gesturing with his hands.

Liam and Anne look each other in the eye and smile at each other. Elizabeth interferes in the matter and says:

"If you two are saying that's how things happened, who are we to doubt it?"

The elderly couple from the “Macaw” base, Mr. Chris Tyler and Mrs. Kelly Tyler, approach William and Emma. Mr. Chris Tyler is a 70-year-old black man, a little fat, with short white hair, while Mrs. Kelly Tyler is a 65-year-old black woman, thin, tall, and with long white hair.

"Mr. Chris Tyler and Mrs. Kelly Tyler," William Thompson said, shaking hands with the elder and greeting him.

"It's been a long time since I last saw him," said Emma Thompson, greeting and kissing the old woman's cheek. "And I see that time has only done you both good."

"Mr. Thompson and Mrs. Thompson!" I'm happy to see you here," says Mr. Chris Tyler, smiling. "And I say the same to you two, it seems that time has not passed for you."

"It is an honor to welcome you here to our humble base," said Mrs. Kelly Tyler, holding Emma's hand. "We've been waiting for all of you for a few days."

Mr. Chris looks at Liam, Anne, Noah, Sophia, Adam, and Elizabeth and then comments:

"I'm also happy to see that the six of you are here safely. I am aware of the participation of all of you in the “Swallow” base against the beasts."

"This is worthy of true 'ALLIANCE WARRIORS”. I'm also very proud of the six of you," says Kelly Tyler, looking at each of the six recruits. "Everyone here at the "Macaw" base knows the story of the "six recruits who faced the beasts that the android ninjas sent."

"The elderly couple, Mr. Henderson and Mrs. Henderson, notified us of the arrival of all of you and notified us of the latest occurrences," warns Mr. Chris Tyler sadly. "Times are hard in all bases of the "ALLIANCE WARRIORS". Both types of androids are evolving their combat strategies, and this is very serious."

Emma clenches her fists, showing that she is outraged by the situation, and speaks:

"These androids cannot continue the way they are. We must do something to reverse this situation."

"We're on our way to resolving this situation against our opponents, my friend," Kelly Tyler says with a smile, pointing to the six recruits and then the other recruits who are on the scene. "As long as there are men and women who believe in the strength of marriage, where two are willing to fight as 'one, ' There will always be hope for a better place."

"As long as there are those who champion the cause, the cause will always exist, and that's what gives us the strength to move forward," said Emma Thompson, perking up, smiling, and looking at Liam, Anne, Noah, Sophia, Adam, and Elizabeth.

"The conversation is very pleasant, but now I want everyone to prepare for the feast I am going to serve, and I will ask them to prepare the rooms," says Mr. Chris Tyler with joy. "Because tomorrow morning we have a lot to do. As they say, "while we breathe, we have to fight for what we believe in."

Emma and William give a thumbs up, and then Mr.

Chris and Mrs. Kelly leave the premises. Emma gestures with one hand, calling Liam, Anne, Noah, Sophia, Adam, and Elizabeth. The six approach Emma and she says:

"William and I are going, because tomorrow morning we will be preparing for another day of training for the recruits and the "ALIANCE WARRIORS". And I don't want the six of you to take too long to go to your lodgings."

"Don't forget that we still have a banquet to go to and I believe someone still needs to talk about the latest events," said William Thompson, smiling and pointing in the direction of David Miller and Lillian Foster, who had just arrived at the venue."

Anne and David run towards each other and hug.

"David!" Anne Smith said with tears in her eyes and smiling. "We are finally together again."

"Anne!" David Miller said with tears streaming down his face and looking into Anne's eyes. "I can't believe you're here."

Anne and David hug each other even tightly. He lifts her up in the air, and David happily spins Anne in the air.

"Don't delay, because, as Mr. Tyler said, 'tomorrow we have a lot to do," warns William Thompson.

"Tomorrow morning we will also resolve the outstanding issues between you recruits for the exchange of training buddies," said Emma Thompson, looking at Liam, Lillian, Anne and David. "The four of you have waited until now, so you can wait a little longer. Be careful."

Emma and William leave the place holding hands. Anne and David continue to embrace.

"How are you, David?" Anne Smith asks, touching David's shoulders, arms, and hands. "I can't believe this is happening."

"Anne, believe me, I'm much better now that I'm with you," David Miller replies, smiling. "And you, how are you?" How have you spent the last few days, my love?"

"I can't describe my feelings of being close to you again, and I want to leave the past in the past."

"You don't know how I waited for this moment. I wanted so badly to leave here to go after you, but they all told me that you were on your way and that there was no need for me to go. I thought about you every day, Anne. Every day, I went to the main gate to see if you arrived."

Lillian approaches Anne and David and says:

"Anne, believe me, when David says he wanted to leave the base to go after you, he really wanted to go after you, the guards were already wanting to arrest him."

"Now I'm here, David, now everything will be different. And when you threw yourself in front of that elephant to save me, I was once again sure that you are my companion for life."

"I would give my life for you if necessary, Anne. You are the woman I want to live the rest of my life with."

Anne and David hug again and even tightly, and look each other in the eyes. Liam, witnessing the situation, has a downcast face and looks at the floor when he sees Anne and David together. Lillian approaches Liam, slaps him lightly on the back, and asks:

"How are you, my future training partner? I say my future training partner because the other recruits have already made the companion changes they had to make. Only the four of us were left to change training partners."

Liam, still dejected, looks at Anne. Anne realizes that

Liam was bothered by the situation and moves away from David a little. David takes Anne's hands and states:

"I don't want to be separated from you ever again, Anne. Never again."

Anne smiles at first, but then stops smiling when she sees that Liam is still bothered by the situation. Liam disguises it when he realizes that Anne is looking at him and says:

"Hello to you too, Lillian. And since everything is solved. Tomorrow we will meet in the teammate exchange area to finalize this pending matter."

"I see that Liam hasn't changed at all," comments Lillian Foster, fiddling with her hair.

"On the contrary, Lillian! Now, Liam is a different person!" says Anne Smith enthusiastically. "He's totally different from old Liam and has changed for the better!"

Noah, Sophia, Adam, Elizabeth, David, and Lillian look in the direction of Anne, who is still very excited.

"It seems like for someone, this adventure was good," comments Lillian Foster, surprised by the situation.

Anne is embarrassed to see that everyone is looking at her, and David doesn't like what he's witnessing at all. David, with a straight face, comments:

"I'm not enjoying this conversation I'm hearing at all."

"Don't worry, David," Liam Cooper said calmly. "Anne and I only got this far because of your willpower to switch training buddies to be with you," he says, looking into Anne's eyes.

Anne looks Liam in the eyes and David holds Anne's hands and laughing, says:

"Now I understand, I was already getting worried. So I just have to thank you, Liam. You brought my saved Anne to me."

"Anne and I just did what we had to do," says Liam Cooper, still looking into Anne's eyes. "You don't have to thank me for that."

"Liam, another thing, I heard about the beast you killed to save Anne," David Miller said, changing his tone to a firmer one. "And I know you only achieved this feat because of her."

"I couldn't have a better explanation than that, because, as I said, Anne and I just did what we had to do," confirms Liam Cooper, making light of the situation, but still looking at Anne.

"But from now on, you can leave it to me, because I'm the one who's going to protect Anne," David Miller says in a serious tone of voice and hugging Anne.

Liam raises his thumb, stops looking at Anne, and slowly moves out of place.

"Liam!" Anne Smith screams.

Liam looks back into Anne's eyes.

"I just wanted to thank you for helping me get here," said Anne Smith, smiling. "We became a great duo at the end of it all."

"You don't need to thank me. I just kept the promise I made to you, nothing more," says Liam Cooper in a sad tone of voice. "See you all tomorrow. I think I need to get some rest now."

"But what about the dinner that's about to be served, Liam?" Adam Scott asks, running his hand over his belly.

"I'm out of appetite," Liam Cooper replies as he

walks.

Noah greets David with a handshake. Anne and Sophia greet Lillian with hugs.

"I'm glad to see that you're safe and well," Noah Cooper said, smiling.

"I say the same, my friend," David Miller said, smiling and giving David a hug.

"Now let's get going, before we miss the time for the banquet," warns Sophia Johnson jokingly. "On the way, I introduce our new friends, Adam Scott and Elizabeth White."

Noah, Anne, David, Lillian, Adam, and Elizabeth agree with Sophia, and the seven recruits go out walking together, talking and playing.

# EVERYTHING IN ITS PROPER PLACE

In the morning, Liam, Anne, Noah, Sophia, William, David, Lillian, Adam, and Elizabeth are in the training partner exchange area. Liam, Anne, David, and Lillian are in their seats, their hands with the bracelet on the device on the table, and waiting for the computer system to finish making the switch.

"The operation of changing training buddies is almost complete," warns William Thompson operating the system that makes the change. "There are a few more minutes left and everything will be in its proper place."

"I didn't have much of a choice, but I'm happy to help my friend, Anne, and her future husband, David," Lillian Foster said, smiling at Anne.

Anne smiles and, with her hand that is not on the exchange device, makes a heart gesture to Lillian. Liam, observing the situation, just lowers his head. Anne, seeing that Liam has a downcast face, stops smiling and focuses on the exchange.

"Liam, once again I want to thank you for what you have done for Anne and for me," David Miller said enthusiastically. "That I will never forget, my friend."

Liam lifts his head and says:

"You don't have to thank me, because, as I said yesterday, Anne and I just did what had to be done."

"Liam, after I heard the whole story of how you all got here, I realized that you've really changed," Lillian Foster says proudly. "I'm impressed and I'm not saying we're a beautiful couple, but we can fight together until we find our destiny."

"Lillian, I tell you I don't want to make the same mistakes as before," says Liam Cooper enthusiastically. "I don't have to throw the weight of my problems on anyone. You can count on me, because this time I'm willing to change and move on," he says, looking at Anne and smiling.

Anne smiles and nods.

"It's hard to believe someone whom you've lost trust," Noah Cooper says with a straight face.

"But this time, I'm going to do it by showing myself that I've changed, not for other people," Liam Cooper says, raising his voice.

Sophia holds Noah's hand and tries to calm the situation between the two brothers. She says:

"It's been a few days since the two of you talked, so we'll leave that for another time and with a friendlier conversation."

"You're right, Sophia, now is not a good time for us to argue," Noah Cooper agrees, letting go of Sophia's hand and walking away from his brother.

"If you stop to analyze, Liam, the plans you had to pursue a life as one of the “Lost”, it was after your partner's betrayal and before you see that Anne and I are an expiration for future couples, so after all that, you really decided to change your projects," explains David Miller in a low voice.

"I appreciate the good example you and Anne are setting for future couples, David," Liam Cooper said sarcastically. "But I just wanted to know how you heard about my story and about 'Lost”.

"Sorry, Liam, I blurted it out, but William and Emma don't know yet," Adam Scott warns in a low voice and gesturing with his hands.

"I hope you stay that way, Adam Scott," Elizabeth White said with a face of few friends.

"Trust me, Liam," Adam Scott said, still apologizing in a low voice. "Not a word more comes out of my mouth on this subject."

"I'm going to remind you to keep your mouth shut on this subject," says Elizabeth White, pulling her companion by the arm. "Let's get out of here, before you end up talking about what you shouldn't be talking about."

"What subject?" William Thompson asks, curious and looking at the recruits. "I want to know about this subject you're talking about."

At first, the eight recruits don't know how to answer and stare at each other without knowing what to do. But then, David takes the initiative and responds:

"The subject is about how difficult his fight was at the "Swallow" base against those lions and hyenas."

William starts joking about the situation and bragging:

"It was a shame that I didn't fight the four felines; these beasts would feel the pressure of my strength if they faced my wife and me."

On the computer screen, a message appears: "PROCESS COMPLETED!".

"Everything is in place now, the exchange of training partners was a success between the four of you," says William Thompson, extending his hugs.

Liam and Lillian leave the table and hold hands. Liam looks at Anne, then looks at Lillian, and in a strong tone of voice, says:

"We're now training partners, Lillian Foster. I will fulfill my role in our partnership as long as we are together."

"Liam Cooper, we are now training partners, and I will do my best as long as we are together," says Lillian Foster in a strong tone of voice.

Anne and David embrace.

"Now everything is as it had to be," says Anne Smith, smiling. "I believe we can now pursue our goal together, David."

"Anne, I'll do anything to make you the happiest woman in the world," says David Miller, putting his hands on Anne's face and looking into her eyes.

The two hug even tighter, and Liam, with a sad face, walks away from the couple.

"How beautiful it is to see love in the air," comments Sophia Johnson with joy.

"I know my brother and I aren't in a very good phase, but I hope he's okay," Noah Cooper comments sadly and looking at Liam. "I noticed that he is trying to be strong and hide what he feels for Anne, but it seems that his feelings are coming out stronger."

"I also hope he gets well and that he finds a great character mate," said Sophia Johnson, looking in Liam's direction and seeing that he is a little dejected by the situation and has his eyes fixed on Anne. "I think these last few days have stirred Liam and Anne's feelings."

"Now we have to give it time for things to fall into place," Noah Cooper said.

Then Emma arrives at the training buddy exchange area and speaks:

"I want everyone's attention! The training is about to

start, and all that's missing is you. We have new resources for training and for real combat. A part of the resources has already been sent to the “Eagle” base and to the “Swallow” base."

Emma shows a transparent capsule of about six inches with a bright orange energy inside.

"Resource capsules!" Noah Cooper said impressed. "That's fantastic!"

"This is amazing!" Sophia Johnson said impressed. "These capsules can help us a lot in battles against androids, as we don't need to recharge the energy of alliances and bracelets in specific locations in the bases, but we can take these capsules with us to recharge our resources in the combat itself."

Emma brings her wedding ring closer to the capsule, and her wedding band absorbs the orange energy from the capsule. Emma, with her wedding ring activates her resources and a new ability option appears written: “Invisibility”.

"We also have capsules with the ability to multiply, fly, climb, among others", explains Emma Thompson, showing other capsules.

William walks in front of the group and turns to everyone, then he looks at Liam, Lillian, Noah, Sophia, David, Anne, Adam, Elizabeth, and finally, he looks at his wife, Emma, and speaks in a strong tone of voice:

"Attention! Our next goals are to dedicate ourselves to training with couples and to dedicate ourselves so that these couples can increase their connections as much as possible."

Emma walks to her husband's side and says:

"We're going to train hard to get stronger and ready for when these androids come back."

William raises his clenched fist and shouts:

"The "ALLIANCE WARRIORS" couples are always ready to fight for the cause!"

Emma, Liam, Lillian, Noah, Sophia, David, Anne, Adam, and Elizabeth raise their arms with closed fists and repeat the same phrase as William:

"The "ALLIANCE WARRIORS" couples are always ready to fight for the cause!"

Then, the ten raise their hands with a closed fist and repeat the phrase once again, and together:

"The "ALLIANCE WARRIORS" couples are always ready to fight for the cause!"

www.ingramcontent.com/pod-product-compliance
Lightning Source LLC
Chambersburg PA
CBHW061057100726
47911CB00012B/281

*9798999425416*